LEARNING CURVE

Much-loved Calleshire research chemist Derek Tridgell has been ill for some time. On his deathbed, his incessant, but unintelligible mutterings culminate in a cry of murder. Detective Inspector Sloan and Detective Constable Crosby are brought in to investigate whether these are just the ramblings of a man at death's door, or a real confession at the final hour. Their enquiries uncover three tragic deaths that may be linked to the deceased's last words: an accidental drowning at a rival chemist manufacturer; an old friend of Derek's killed in a caving expedition; his son walking away unscathed from a fatal car accident. It's a complex case for Sloan and Crosby.

LEARNING CURVE

LEARNING CURVE

by

Catherine Aird

Magna Large Print Books
Long Preston, North Yorkshire,
BD23 4ND, England.

British Library Cataloguing in Publication Data.

A catalogue record of this book is
available from the British Library

ISBN   978-0-7505-4538-9

First published in Great Britain by Allison & Busby in 2016

Published in Large Print 2018 by arrangement with
Allison & Busby Ltd.

Magna Large Print is an imprint of Library Magna Books Ltd.

Printed and bound in Great Britain by
T.J. (International) Ltd., Cornwall, PL28 8RW

For
Andrew, Alex, Angelina and Sebastiano
with love

CHAPTER ONE

'Is it all right to come in, Mum?' called out the girl anxiously as she hurried up the flight of stairs towards her parents' bedroom. She pushed open the door without waiting for an answer, asking through lips unusually dry, 'How is he?'

'Much the same, dear,' answered Marion Tridgell, her mother, quietly. This wasn't strictly true – the man in the bed was clearly sinking – but his wife didn't want to put the fact into words. That would have meant recognising the reality of his impending death, and this was something Marion Tridgell wasn't quite ready to do.

Not just yet.

'Is he still talking as much as he was?' enquired Jane Tridgell, reluctantly making her gaze travel in the direction of the familiar figure of her father. He was propped up against the pillows in his bed, his face an unhealthy shade of grey tinged with bright yellow, his skin stretched tautly over the bone structure of his face, and his breathing laboured.

'He is,' sighed the man's wife.

'Poor old Dad,' murmured Jane. Until now her conception of dying had been based on Sir Anthony van Dyck's highly stylised painting, all white lace and jewellery, entitled *Venetia, Lady Digby, on her Deathbed*. Not any more. Now it was Nicolas Poussin's painting *Extreme Unction* that

11

flooded into her memory, the distraught wife and daughter at a bedside as the priest anoints the eyes of the dying man in the centre of the picture. She had begun to study art at college and had already started to see the world through its prism. Only now she was beginning to discover that art wasn't quite the same as life.

'Ninety to the dozen,' sighed Marion Tridgell, her own face like her husband's, quite pale and drawn, too. 'But I still can't make out what about.' She was sitting on a chair placed by his bedside, stroking his face from time to time with the lightest of touches.

As deathbeds went, this one had appeared ordinary enough to everyone around it, everyone, that is, except the patient's daughter, Jane. She hadn't encountered death before and everything about it was very new and strange to her and quite unlike what she had read in fiction. There was, though, one feature about it that seemed different to all the dying man's family, although it was one thing that nobody else seemed to find at all out of the ordinary.

Derek Tridgell just wouldn't stop talking.

'But what exactly is he saying?' asked Jane – and not for the first time. Her father had been gabbling away for days now.

'And,' said Marion, herself quite mystified, 'who on earth is he talking to? That's what I would like to know. Not me, anyway. That's for sure.' There was a quaver in her voice when she added, 'He doesn't even know who I am any more.'

'He's talking to someone neither of us know anyway,' said Jane decisively, moving to put her arms round her mother. 'I'm sure about that, unless, Mum, you know someone called the remainderman.'

Her mother shook her head. 'I've never heard the word before.'

'Me neither,' said Jane.

Marion Tridgell, markedly anxious, said in a choked voice, 'I keep telling Dr Browne about your father's talking so much but he just says not to worry about it. Some patients do at this stage, he says. It's the drugs.'

Jane moved swiftly round the room to the other side of her father's bed and put her ear close to his mouth; today she could only catch – but not understand – the odd word. She was the person to whom this death – any death – didn't seem ordinary simply because she hadn't seen any human being so near to the end of his or her life before.

'I do wish, though, that I knew what he was talking about, let alone who he was talking to,' said Marion in a strained voice. 'You listen again, Jane, and see if you can tell me what's weighing so much on his poor, sick mind. Nobody else seems able to.'

The deathbed had seemed ordinary enough, pedestrian even, to all those professionals visiting the dying man's bedroom at Legate Lodge in the Calleshire village of Friar's Flensant who had had some previous acquaintance with death or, rather, with the process of dying. This naturally included the visiting doctor who had tried to convey to the family the difference between postponing death and prolonging the act of dying. Dr Angus Browne had chosen his words to the relatives with a skill

13

honed from long practice.

'Your husband shouldn't be in any discomfort now, Mrs Tridgell,' the doctor had said on his latest visit as he had begun to repack his bag, after noting the patient's advanced cachexia and giving him a particularly large injection of painkiller, 'but let me know if he seems to be in any way really distressed.'

If asked – but only if asked – the general practitioner could have gone on to explain the so-called double effect of the drugs he was administering – in that they killed the pain all right but at the risk of killing the patient, too – but he saw no good would come of doing so at this particular stage.

And, more importantly, the family hadn't asked him.

At the time Marion Tridgell had nodded her total understanding of what he had been telling her. She was one of those coming and going in the bedroom mature enough and experienced enough to have seen death before and importantly knew what to say and what to leave unsaid. She had glanced towards her husband in the bed and said to Dr Browne, 'Derek's still talking nonsense, though, Doctor. We can't understand it at all. He keeps going on about someone called the remainderman. The wrong remainderman, whoever that is.'

'It happens sometimes,' said the doctor sagely. 'The mind's a funny thing as death approaches and we have no means of knowing what any patient is thinking at this stage. Nobody has.'

'He keeps on saying the same thing over and over again, though, as if there's something worry-

14

ing him,' persisted Mrs Tridgell.

'And is there anything you know of that he was particularly worried about?' asked the doctor, unconsciously using the past tense.

She shook her head. 'No, Doctor. We can't imagine what on earth he's talking about because no one can quite catch his words. It's only now and then there's one that makes sense.'

'It's probably not too important – I shouldn't let it worry you,' said the doctor kindly, snapping his bag closed and taking his leave. 'Do try to get some sleep yourself if you can.' The words 'While you can', he left unsaid.

The patient's daughter, Jane, had sniffed when she had been told what the doctor had said. 'That's all very well for him to say that but I think whatever it is about, it's worrying Dad. He sounds to me very upset about something.'

'But we don't know what,' seconded her mother. 'I have no idea who or what the wrong remainder-man is but Dad's certainly talking to someone.'

'Someone who isn't here,' pointed out Jane astringently.

'Paul, you mean?' said Marion, adjusting her husband's oxygen mask a little as she spoke. Paul was Jane's brother, and the son of the increasingly breathless man on the bed.

'Yes.'

Marion shook her head. 'No, I'm sure it's not Paul he's talking to.'

'So where exactly has my dear brother got to now?' Jane asked impatiently.

'All I know is that he's well on his way to the airport. He rang about an hour ago.'

15

'Where from this time?'

'He's still in Brazil,' replied Marion, defensively. Her son, a dropout from university and two jobs, was something of a nomad, always moving to one country after another in search of a better life, which he still hadn't yet found.

'He couldn't be much further away when he's wanted, could he?'

'I've told you, dear, that he's been keeping in touch on his mobile whenever he could get a signal,' said Marion. 'You know what he's like.'

'And how,' said Paul's younger sister unsympathetically.

'He says he's not far from the nearest airport now, wherever that is. Rio de Janeiro, I think. He's promised he'll get there as soon as he possibly can and catch the first plane out.'

Jane was tempted to ask if Paul had been stuck up a creek without a paddle again since this had literally once happened to him on a tributary of the River Amazon but she didn't. Instead she murmured something about hoping that he would get here in time. What she was actually thinking was that a banshee would have come in handy. A female Irish spirit giving a shriek just before a death in the family would have been very useful at this point.

'I hope he does, too,' said Paul's mother sincerely, 'for his sake as well as ours, but Dr Browne says we've just got to let nature take its course now.'

'Perhaps Dad's ramblings will mean something to Paul when he gets here,' suggested Jane doubtfully.

'I would like to hope so because they certainly don't mean anything to me and it would help,' said Marion, very near to tears now. She lifted her head. 'Listen, Dad's started talking again. You see if you can understand what he's saying.'

Jane bent down over the bed and put her ear to the patient's mouth, listening intently. After a while she reported, 'I think that what he keeps on saying is that he's coming as soon as he can. And that someone's got to wait for him.'

'But coming where?' asked the other woman.

'Search me. I don't know. All I can say is that it seems very odd to me,' murmured Jane, who thought she could guess where it was her dying father meant he was coming to but she didn't like to say.

The next world.

But where in the next world Jane did not know. Heaven and Hell were just abstract concepts in her philosophy – however imaginatively the artists she was studying depicted them. Her father, although something of an old-fashioned churchman, had never been one to talk about his beliefs to her. And, she thought ruefully, it was too late now to explore the subject.

Suddenly the sick man became more audible and announced quite clearly again to some unknown person, 'I'm coming. I'm nearly there now.'

Before the mother and daughter could do more than exchange puzzled glances, two young carers came into the bedroom. The deathbed had seemed quite ordinary to them, practised as they were at attending them. They had come and gone to the house throughout the last few weeks but then they had treated everyone – including the patient – with a cheerful over-familiarity that the family found irksome and intrusive but were too polite and preoccupied to remonstrate about with them.

That these girls were more sensitive than they were given credit for had become apparent as Derek Tridgell had inched his way towards his necessary end. Since then and as time went on, they had increasingly tempered their attempts to amuse the patient. Weeks had passed now since they had last gone in for the gallows humour of such remarks to him as 'If you wake up dead, I'll kill you.' It had amused the patient greatly then – but that was then, not now. And today as swiftly as they had come, they were gone, leaving their patient comfortable and the bedclothes tidy.

There had been other visitors, too, but only at the beginning of his illness. Preoccupied as she was, Marion had registered the different approaches they had made to the ill man. Jonathon Sharp, the head of the firm where the patient worked, Berebury Pharmaceuticals, had called more than once, delivered a bit of harmless shop talk and gone on his way. At that stage Derek Tridgell had been quite happy to talk.

'Anything more on that ghastly accident at Luston Chemicals, Jonathon?' he had asked on one of his visits.

'Nothing definite,' said his boss.

Tridgell shuddered. 'I'm sure that Michael Linane was the man behind all our troubles with Ameliorite, seeing as he is – was – their head of sales.'

'So am I, although I don't know that we could ever prove it.' Sharp nodded in tacit agreement. 'Difficult thing to try to do anyway now in view of what happened and his chairman isn't going to help us one little bit.'

'Ralph Iddon's only interested in Luston Chemicals – I've said that all along.' Tridgell waved a thin, wasted, hand. 'It might just have saved our bacon, though, that man Linane dying when he did.'

'I sure hope that it has,' said the chairman firmly, 'although I wouldn't wish dying like that on my worst enemy.'

'I wonder what will happen now,' mused Tridgell, who didn't want to talk about modes of dying just then.

'I think it's too soon to say,' the chairman hedged. 'All the same, I wish we hadn't gone over there that particular day. Apart from anything else, it was a complete waste of time.' Like all businessmen, Jonathon Sharp cherished his time as if it was his working capital, which perhaps it was. 'And,' he snorted, 'they weren't going to play fair with their precious product Mendaner whatever we offered. I'm sure about that.'

'Damn silly name for a drug,' pronounced Derek Tridgell. 'It sounds like one of those funny bicycles that they used to call a Neracar. Or was it a tricycle?'

'I'm afraid time alone will tell what will happen in the end,' said the chairman, some of whose skill lay in taking the long view and the rest in ignoring irrelevances.

Derek had smiled weakly at that and said, 'And

I'll never know, will I?'

Or will I? He had asked himself when his boss had gone but, unsurprisingly, there came no answer.

His old friend and caving companion, Simon Thornycroft, had come to see him too. 'Amelia sent her best wishes,' Simon said, 'and if there's anything either of us can do, you know you only have to say.'

Derek Tridgell had nodded then, this action sometimes being easier than talking with a mouth made increasingly dry by analgesics.

'The whole club's thinking of you,' Thornycroft went on.

Tridgell tried to moisten his lips. 'What did the lads try at the weekend?'

'The Hawecroft Chimney.'

'Get anywhere?'

Simon Thornycroft grimaced. 'Only about half-way up. It's just a bit too wide for comfort and we haven't any ladders long enough. Not yet, anyway.'

The ill man raised an enfeebled hand and said in a weak voice, 'You'll get to the top one day, Simon. Not in my time, though.'

His visitor, embarrassed, ignored this last remark and said instead, 'The opening must be grassed over. I reckon we'll only find it when a cow falls through the turf and lets in a bit of light.'

'Good luck, anyway,' Tridgell managed to say through his drug-dried lips.

There was an awkward silence between the two men and then Simon Thornycroft coughed and said hesitantly, 'The club is thinking of naming that new ghyll we've found after you, old man.'

'Very kind of them,' said Derek, 'but any memorial ought to be to poor Edmund Leaton. You know that.'

A shadow passed over the other man's face. He winced as he said, 'It's Amelia who doesn't want that. Not me. She can't bear to think of his death. Not even now.'

Just then the patient's wife, Marion, appeared at the bedroom door, bringing the visit to an end. It was impossible to tell whether the patient was pleased or not about this. Marion thought her husband was now beyond caring about anything in this world but nevertheless she thanked Simon Thornycroft warmly as he went upon his way.

The vicar's approach had been tentative and tactful. 'I thought I'd just look in and see how things were,' said the Reverend Mr Derek Tompkinson. Friar's Flensant was one of the half a dozen small parishes in his care in this rural part of the Calleshire diocese and he was a conscientious man.

'Going south,' said Derek. 'And quite quickly now.'

The vicar didn't attempt to deny this. 'But you're not in pain, I hope.'

'Not yet,' said the patient grimly.

'I shouldn't worry too much about that if I were you. The doctors have a lot of shots in their lockers these days.'

'So they keep telling me,' said the patient.

The clergyman sat in companionable silence beside his parishioner until it was broken – as he had known it would be – by Derek Tridgell. 'I want to be buried,' he said suddenly. 'Not cremated.'

'Right.'

'And I'd like a muffled peal of bells at the funeral.'

'I won't forget,' the vicar promised.

Derek stirred. 'And proper hymns. No need for the choir, though.'

The other man smiled. The church choir wasn't what it had been. 'I know exactly what you mean.'

'What I really want, though, now, Vicar, between you and me and the gatepost is for someone to – what did that poet fellow say? "Let me go".'

'He will, I promise you.' The vicar rose, and touching the man's shoulder lightly in passing, said, 'God bless you.'

There had been no visitors admitted to the sickroom for several days now and Marion was glad. She didn't have to be polite and welcoming any more. Or preternaturally self-controlled.

Abruptly now the attention of both Derek Tridgell's wife and daughter was again caught by a voice coming from the bed. 'Dammit, dammit, dammit,' the dying man said loudly and clearly. 'For God's sake, dammit.'

Jane ventured a wry grimace. 'I must say that's not like Dad. He can usually manage something a bit stronger than dammit.'

'He's not himself,' said Marion unnecessarily.

Her daughter managed a faint smile. 'You can say that again, Mum.'

The man in the bed suddenly became increasingly agitated, his voice taking on an urgent, pleading note. Now Derek Tridgell was staring, his eyes unfocused, into the distance. He said, 'I'm coming, man. Wait for me. I'm on my way.'

'It happens, Mrs Tridgell.' The community nurse, older and more experienced than the care assistants, had been a frequent visitor to the bedroom, and had been reassuring about the patient's continual talking. 'You mustn't let it worry you.'

The deathbed had seemed ordinary enough to the visiting nurse, too, she having seen it all before, but she was old enough now to have begun to think about her own end. A single woman, she knew she wasn't going to be surrounded by any genuinely grieving relatives at hers. The Tridgell family would have been very surprised to learn that in some ways she envied them. There would be no loving kindness evident at her solitary demise. Professional to the last, though, she had always done what she had come to do and then left, displacing all thoughts about herself as she did so by concentrating instead on her next visit.

Derek lay quiet and apparently calm for so long after the carers had gone that day that Jane said, 'What about a cup of tea, Mum?'

'I'd love one, dear.'

'And something to eat?'

'I don't think I could manage anything just now, thank you. I'm not hungry.'

'I'll be back in a jiffy,' she promised. When she came back with a pot of tea on a tray she said, 'I cleared the answerphone while I was waiting for the kettle, Mum.'

'Thank you, dear.' Marion had only answered the telephone when it had been her son on the

23

line, there being no one else to whom she had wanted to speak at this time.

'Kate Booth sent good wishes from all the cavers, so did someone from the firm – I've forgotten who – Jonathon himself, I think it might have been but his voice wasn't very clear – and Amelia Thornycroft sent her love and said she and Simon were thinking of us and if there was anything at all we wanted we were to say.'

'That was nice of them,' said her mother absently, not really listening.

'And,' here Jane's voice quavered a little, 'the man from Barnett's said that lawnmower's been serviced and is ready to be picked up.' The lawns at Legate Lodge had been Derek Tridgell's pride and joy, always carefully trimmed, but they were already showing signs of neglect. Jane was surprised to discover how much she minded about this.

'Paul can see to cutting the grass when he gets back,' said Marion absently.

Suppressing her immediate response that chance would be a fine thing, Paul having to her certain knowledge never having handled the lawnmower in his life, Jane set about pouring the tea. It was then that a change came over her father. He suddenly sat bolt upright in the bed and announced in a loud and clear voice, 'He did it, you know.'

'Did what, dear?' asked Marion, investing her words with a great tenderness that she hoped would get through to her dying husband.

'Killed him, of course,' announced Derek Tridgell loudly, giving a shuddering gasp and then falling back on his pillows, quite dead.

CHAPTER TWO

'It's not exactly a great deal to go on, sir, is it?' ventured Detective Inspector Sloan. 'Something a dying man is said to have cried out at the moment of death.'

'But whichever way you look at it, Sloan,' pronounced Superintendent Leeyes grandly, 'what the deceased did say just might be a genuine reference to a killing and therefore we can't ignore it.'

'No, sir. Of course not, sir.'

'However much we might like to,' added the superintendent more realistically. 'Remember, a man's last words are considered to be the truth.'

The two policemen were at the headquarters of 'F' Division of the Calleshire County Constabulary. These were in the market town of Berebury where Detective Inspector Christopher Dennis Sloan, who was known as 'Seedy' to his family and friends, was head of the force's tiny Criminal Investigation Department. Such crime as there was in the eastern half of the county – save on the highway – usually ended up on his desk.

'I don't think, sir, that we've got any unsolved murders on our patch,' said Sloan, adding cautiously, 'that is, of course, any ones that we actually know about.'

'That doesn't mean that there aren't any at all,' countered Leeyes briskly. 'There could be any number of accidents and suicides that weren't what they were said to be.'

'On the other hand, sir, even if we had some on the books, so to speak, and were able to solve one of them, the court couldn't very well convict on the spoken evidence of the dead man since he can't be cross-questioned. You can't even libel the dead,' he added irrelevantly, a little bit of common law coming back to him.

'We could clear up a case, Sloan. That would be good,' said Leeyes.

'Naturally, sir,' said Sloan smoothly, ignoring this volte-face on the part of the superintendent who usually had no time for criminal statistics.

Or, come to that, the past.

'It would go down well,' mused Leeyes, his own track record always a matter of great importance to him. 'Clearing up an old case, I mean. Quite the done thing these days, DNA being what it is.'

'Quite so, sir,' Sloan said, trying to recollect who it was in history whose body had been dug up in order to be hanged by revisionists, a later mob wanting its pound of flesh. Had it been the late Oliver Cromwell, dead of disease, who had been so treated for past misdemeanours reconsidered by history? He couldn't remember. 'That is, if the person who committed the crime is still alive and we are able to get a conviction without the testimony of the deceased, to say nothing of any DNA.'

'Even so,' agreed the superintendent after some little thought, 'I don't see how we could very well have a trial with a dead witness.'

'Quite, sir,' said Sloan, although he knew there were benighted regimes where this did happen.

26

But then he knew, too, that once upon a time animals had been tried in this country for the murder of other animals: he reminded himself that therefore it didn't do to be patronising of other nations – or of what had happened in the past either.

'Even though we would know where to find the accuser,' said the superintendent, heavily humorous. 'He'll be in the cemetery by then.'

'Presumably there hasn't been time for him to have been buried yet?' said Sloan. He hoped that it was interment the family of the late Derek Tridgell were indeed planning. The superintendent didn't like cremations, preferring the remains to be available to be seen both now and in the future should it ever become necessary.

The superintendent shook his head. 'No, not yet, Sloan, although apparently the doctor is quite prepared to issue a death certificate for the deceased since there is no doubt about the cause of his death – I'm told it was pancreatic cancer. I understand the family are awaiting the return of the deceased's son from South America before they start to arrange the funeral.'

'The only doubt, then, sir, seems to be about the death which the deceased declared at the point of his own demise that someone else, unnamed, had brought about,' sighed Sloan, as he tried to encapsulate the problem as it affected the police and leaving aside the intriguing question of whether murderers could now be buried in consecrated ground. 'I suppose the late Derek Tridgell didn't by any chance say how this unknown someone had killed someone else equally unknown?'

27

'No, all that the two women said he did talk about was somebody called the remainderman. That word mean anything to you, Sloan?'

'No, sir.' He took a deep breath and, getting back to the matter in hand, pointed out carefully, 'So, sir, all we can say for certain is that it was a very nearly dead man talking.'

He had decided against discussing with his superior officer exactly what constituted a killing since all the legal eagles he knew were prepared to debate the definition ad infinitum. Besides which, in his experience, every motorist he had ever known who had been at the wheel in a fatal accident – and that was a killing if ever there was one – found it difficult to forget for the rest of their lives, and that was whether guilty or not, and whether convicted or not.

'It's what the man said that's important, Sloan,' the superintendent reminded him reproachfully, 'and precisely when he said it.'

'Yes, sir,' said Sloan, making a mental note to look up the validity of deathbed confessions. He thought he remembered that that which was spoken in imminent expectation of death by the deceased came into a category all of its own in criminal law. He would have to think about this.

The superintendent adjusted the message sheet on his desk in front of him and read it out aloud. 'The man's wife – his widow now, of course – and his daughter were both present in the room at the time and heard him quite clearly say someone had killed someone.'

'But not who or how?' asked Sloan hopefully, although two witnesses were always better than one, unless their testimony differed.

Or, perhaps, even if it did.

Perhaps especially, then.

'I'm afraid not, Sloan. They say that he then fell back on the bed without speaking again and was confirmed as dead very soon after by their general practitioner.'

'Is that all the evidence we have, sir? If I may say so, it doesn't seem to amount to a great deal.'

'And I'm afraid they said he'd been talking nonsense for quite a while before he died,' said Leeyes, glancing down again at a message sheet on his desk.

'So what we don't know, I take it, sir,' said Sloan, 'is whether this statement was nonsense, too.'

'Exactly, Sloan.'

'Then I'd better try and find out what the patient had been prescribed in the way of medication first,' said Sloan. No policeman needed to be reminded of what some drugs did to the human mind. 'And get some witness statements.'

'Witness statements, Sloan,' barked the superintendent severely, 'which I must remind you that we can't ignore and mustn't put on the back-burner.'

'Of course not, sir,' said Sloan virtuously. He wasn't sure whether or not in this instance witness statements would come into the category of circumstantial evidence. It was too soon to say.

'And, Sloan,' went on the superintendent, 'don't forget that the two women's accounts of what was said agree in every particular. So far,' he added lugubriously.

Sloan suppressed an automatic rejoinder that

this could also mean collusion: or that mother and daughter might have had an agenda all of their own. Instead he asked if the two women had also both agreed to the police being told about the dying man's last words or just one of them had insisted on it. 'Since if they hadn't, sir, we wouldn't have known anything about what had been said, would we?'

Sloan thought that fact was interesting in itself and tucked it away in the back of his mind.

'I couldn't begin to say about that, Sloan.' Leeyes pushed a piece of paper towards him. 'All we've got to go on so far is the message we had from the daughter.'

'I still wonder why they told us?' mused Detective Inspector Sloan aloud, reaching for his notebook. 'I'd better have the wife's name and address.'

'Marion Tridgell, of Legate Lodge, High Street, Friar's Flensant.'

'And the daughter's?'

'Jane, of that ilk and address,' said the superintendent. 'She's an art student,' he added in a tone of voice that could only be called condemnatory.

'Right, sir. I'll get on to them straightaway.' There was other work on his desk awaiting his attention – an outbreak of more petty theft in Cullingoak and a case of serious fraud in Almstone to say nothing of what looked suspiciously like a Ponzi scheme at Pelling – but they would have to wait until he had reported back to the superintendent. He knew that.

'And it would be a great help,' added Leeyes, heavily sarcastic, 'if you would be so kind as to take Detective Constable Crosby out to Friar's Flensant with you and therefore out of my sight.'

'Sir?' said Sloan. Detective Constable Crosby, the most jejune recruit to the division, was not an asset in any investigation but he was usually kept at a safe distance from the superintendent.

'He tore a strip off a man who was in a car using my reserved parking place at the station yesterday...' said Leeyes.

'But, sir...' began Sloan, since the superintendent's reserved parking place at the police station was the nearest thing to hallowed ground that he knew.

'But the man in the car was doing it by prior arrangement with me, seeing that he was one of Her Majesty's Inspectors of Constabulary,' snarled Superintendent Leeyes.

A loud clatter at the front door of Legate Lodge at Friar's Flensant heralded Paul Tridgell's arrival home. He stepped in through the doorway at the same time as letting his rucksack slip off his shoulders with audible relief. It landed with a noisy bump on the floor of the hall.

Marion Tridgell hurried forward and greeted him with a little hug of welcome. He put his arms round his mother's shoulders and squeezed them gently. He was dishevelled from lack of sleep and badly in need of a shave. 'Sorry to be too late, Mum,' he said. 'I did try.'

'I know you did, dear.' Marion gave her son another hug, 'but South America's a long way away. I know that.'

'And I was up country, which didn't help.' He

31

shrugged his shoulders. 'Besides, I hadn't realised poor old Dad was quite so ill.'

'I'm not sure that any of us did to begin with,' said his mother sadly. 'I don't think I quite took in what the doctor was telling me at the time. One doesn't, you know. Anyway, I know Dad would have quite understood.'

Paul looked back over his shoulder as there was a knock at the front door behind him. 'Oh, I forgot. Mum, can you rustle up the taxi fare? I haven't got any English money on me.'

As his mother went to get her handbag, he called after her, 'Where's Jane?'

'Making tea.' She gave a shaky laugh as she came back, purse in hand. 'Drink tea – that's all either of us seem to have been able to do since – well, you know.' Mother and son nodded their complete mutual understanding: it didn't need speech.

'I know. I'm not hungry either,' he said, giving a great stretch. 'What I really need now is a bath and a shave. Let me pay the driver and then I'll go and give Jane a hand with the tray.'

After paying the taxi driver, Paul made his way into the kitchen and greeted his sister. 'Hi, Jane, I'm back at last.'

'Hi,' she said, notably low-key and busying herself over the kettle.

'Sorry and all that – about not being here.'

Jane passed a hand over tired eyes. 'Honestly, Paul, I don't think it would have made any difference if you had been so I shouldn't worry about it if I were you. Dad didn't even know Mum at the end, let alone me. It was awful.'

'Tell me,' he said.

'Oh, Paul,' she sighed. 'Poor Dad. You mightn't even have recognised him if you had got back in time. I couldn't believe that he could have looked as wizened and old as he did when he died. He was yellow all over, too.'

'But he wasn't old, was he? I mean not really old. And he was so fit and active, too.'

'Squash and speleology,' she said. 'That's what he always said kept him fit. Although Dr Browne did say we should remember that being fit and being healthy were two very different things.'

'Good thinking.' He went on awkwardly, 'You know I wouldn't have stayed away for so long if he'd been really old. You know that. Or if I'd known how very ill he was. Mum didn't tell me, not properly, until last week that he was actually dying. You know what she's like.'

She nodded. 'I know she didn't want to worry you. But that wasn't it.'

'No?'

'No. The worst part was that towards the end Dad just wouldn't stop talking.'

'What on earth about?' Her brother stared at her and listened to her account of their father's last days. Then he said with elaborate casualness, 'Was he talking about anything particular? While he still could, I mean.'

'He talked all the time, although we weren't sure what it was all about,' she said. 'That was what was so funny. Then he started to go on about someone called the remainderman being wrong, if you know what on earth that means.'

Paul Tridgell wrinkled his nose. In one of his many attempts to find a career which he liked, let

33

alone one to which he was suited, Paul had briefly worked in a bank. 'If I remember rightly, the remainderman's the person who gets the dibs in the end – however many other people have had their hands on it along the way. To put it another way: in the long run, the survivor wins.'

'The last man standing, I suppose you might call it,' she said thoughtfully.

'Or he who laughs last laughs longest,' said her brother, more cynically.

'So who could the wrong remainderman be?'

'Search me.' He gave a prodigious yawn. 'Actually, it's a bit like a tontine used to be but they're not legal any more. Too many people got knocked off in the process.'

'What he was saying didn't mean a thing to me or Mum,' she said, putting a milk jug on a tray, adding, 'Neither does a tontine for that matter.'

'Here, I'll carry that,' he said, moving forward. 'Did he say anything really important?'

She lifted her head at that. 'What do you mean exactly?'

'Any last wishes, fond farewells – that sort of thing?'

'Yes, since you ask. But unexpected.'

'What?'

'Something very odd.'

Paul clenched his fists until the knuckles were quite white. 'Tell me.'

Jane spoke slowly and carefully. 'Just before he died, Dad announced quite loudly and clearly, "He killed him, you know."'

'His exact words?'

She nodded, filling the teapot from the steaming kettle and putting it on a tray already laid with cups and saucers.

'Nothing else?'

'Nothing,' she said. 'And then he died.'

'Just like that?'

She nodded again. 'So we told the police.'

'You did what!' he exploded, suddenly white-faced.

'Told the police,' she repeated. 'Look out, Paul, you're spilling the milk.'

'Why on earth did you want to go and do that for?'

'Mum and I thought about it for a bit and we decided we should. And,' she added in a tone entirely devoid of inflexion, 'you weren't here to ask.'

'No need to remind me.'

'After all,' she said, 'it wasn't as if Dad himself had said that he'd killed anyone.'

'But you thought the police ought to know that he had said somebody did,' he echoed in a bitter voice.

'That's right, Paul,' she said flatly, 'Mum and I thought they ought to know and they've told us they're on their way over here now. Like it or not,' she added.

CHAPTER THREE

'Where to, sir?' asked Detective Constable Crosby. He had brought the police car round to the door and was waiting there as Sloan stepped out of the police station. The constable was standing poised alongside the car rather in the manner of a Grand Prix driver ready for the off.

Detective Inspector Sloan pulled out his note-book and read out the address, 'Legate Lodge, High Street, Friar's Flensant.' Friar's Flensant was just one of the many small villages in the hinter-land of the market town of Berebury, home of 'F' Division of the Calleshire County Constabulary.

'Not far, then,' said Crosby, slipping the car into gear. 'And it won't take long to get out there seeing as it's not market day.' Market day meant a square full of stalls and people, not roads and cars.

'I'm sorry to disappoint you, Crosby,' said Sloan, 'but I'm afraid that time is not of the essence in this instance. At least,' he added fairly, 'not in the usual sense.'

'Right, sir.'

The inspector strapped himself into the pas-senger seat and sat back. 'We are going to visit what I assume to be a house of mourning.'

'So there's been a death, sir,' concluded Crosby.

'True but that is not the point. The question is whether there have been two deaths.'

'A double murder?' The constable brightened and unconsciously put his foot down.

'No, Crosby. There has been one death that we do know about and wasn't murder and one that we know nothing whatsoever about but might have been. That is, if it happened at all. All we have to go on is just something that the late Derek Tridgell is said to have uttered just before he died.'

'A swansong?'

'You could call it that, Crosby.'

'Canaries sing, too, sir, don't they?' said Crosby, who was still learning the criminal argot.

'Only if they're ready to watch their backs for the rest of what's left of their lives,' said Sloan, older and wiser.

'A deathbed confession, then?' suggested Crosby.

'On the contrary, Crosby.' That was one thing that he thought he could be sure about. 'It seems it's more of a deathbed accusation.'

'Then why didn't he tell us before?' asked Crosby indignantly, 'then we could have asked him all about it.'

'Perhaps that's exactly why,' murmured Sloan. 'It could also have been something that was weighing on his mind which he had been concentrating on keeping back until he couldn't restrain himself any longer.'

'More canary than swan, though,' said the constable, pleased with the thought.

'Could be. Or it might just have been that he couldn't control his own mind any more, the effect of drugs being what they are. He was very near death indeed when he spoke. They were his last words, in fact.'

'Nice timing, then,' observed the constable, slowing down as the car trickled into the village high street at Friar's Flensant. 'Ruled himself out of play.'

'Beyond our reach, anyway,' agreed Detective Inspector Sloan, looking around. 'There's the house – over there, beyond the post office.'

The constable drew the police car up in front of a neat square dwelling, its red brick set off well by white-painted windows and a front door with old-fashioned brass fittings. 'Nice,' he observed approvingly. 'Garden in quite good nick, too.'

'And designed to be labour-saving,' noted Sloan, a gardener himself whenever he got the time, 'although the lawn could do with a trim. You can hardly see the Wembley lines any longer but they've been there all right.'

'Come again, sir?'

'Grass properly mown in straight lines,' said Sloan briefly. What he was trying to decide was whether or not to prime the young constable on their forthcoming interview strategy. He decided against it. Letting nature take its course sometimes worked out better.

Jane Tridgell admitted the two policemen to Legate Lodge and led the way to a room where her mother was sitting, silent and still. She stirred as the officers came in, moving slowly, though, and as if movement was a great effort. She indicated a young man lounging on a sofa. 'And this is my son, Paul.'

Paul Tridgell nodded at the policemen but did

not get to his feet.

'We weren't sure if we should have bothered the police at all,' Mrs Tridgell began apologetically, 'but it seemed such a strange thing for my husband to have said and we thought we would have only worried afterwards if we hadn't told you.'

'Waste of police time, if you ask me,' yawned the young man on the sofa.

'There's a lot of that about,' contributed Detective Constable Crosby. 'Mostly old ladies who've lost their cats. Or their marbles.'

'So we thought you ought to know,' put in Jane Tridgell, who had come in quietly behind them and taken a seat next to her mother. She ignored what her brother had said. 'Of course, it might just have been something and nothing. We know that.'

'But it might not,' agreed Detective Inspector Sloan.

'You can't be serious,' said Paul.

'We take everything seriously, sir,' said Sloan.

'But it could mean nothing at all,' he persisted.

'Very true, sir. Equally it might mean something,' said Sloan mildly. 'And we need to know which, so please do go on, Miss Tridgell.'

Jane dutifully told him exactly what her father had said. The detective inspector listened carefully to all that she told him.

'And you have no idea who he meant when he talked about the remainderman?' he said. '"The wrong remainderman", I think you said.'

'None,' she replied.

'Or why he should say "dammit" so often and so forcefully?'

39

She shook her head. 'Neither of us have.'

'Was this a normal expletive of his?'

'No, Inspector.' A little smile played around her lips. 'His were usually a bit stronger.'

'Much stronger,' said the young man on the sofa. 'Dad had a good command of language.'

'But he said nothing more?' Sloan asked when he had finished writing his notes.

'Then he just died,' she said lamely.

'Confession is good for the soul,' remarked Paul from the sofa. 'But not a lot else.'

'Paul,' his mother corrected him sharply, 'your father didn't say he'd killed someone but that someone else had.'

'Sounds to me as if it was something he wanted to get off his chest anyway,' said Paul, 'and if that's not a confession then I don't know what is.'

Sloan turned to him. 'Did you hear any of this, too, sir?'

'Me? No, I was in the air on the way home from Rio de Janeiro. Red eye isn't in it. I came straight here but I was too late.' He hitched himself up on a shoulder. 'And I've got my airline ticket stub to prove it.'

'I'm sure that won't be necessary, sir, thank you.' He turned back to Marion Tridgell and her daughter and said, 'So may I take it that neither of you has any idea what he was talking about?'

Both women shook their heads.

Sloan turned to Paul. 'Or you, sir?'

'Nope,' said Paul. 'No skeletons in the family cupboard that I know about – or at least,' he looked across at his mother, 'that anyone has told me about.'

40

'Or outside the family?' asked Sloan, unamused.

They all shook their heads. Then, after a moment, Paul frowned and said, 'There was someone who was killed in a firm Dad knew about, wasn't there? He always said that it was an industrial accident but you never know.'

'Where was that?' asked Sloan.

'Luston Chemicals,' said Marion. 'They make the same sort of things that my husband's – my late husband's – employer produced.'

'Only they're bigger,' put in Paul. 'Much bigger.'

'A man did die over there,' said his mother. 'It was all very unfortunate.'

'When exactly?' asked Sloan.

She shook her head. 'I'm sorry, Inspector, I can't remember when exactly – a year or so ago, perhaps. I've found time a bit telescoped since my husband became ill – but I do remember him talking about it.'

'He talked about it quite a lot,' put in Paul vigorously. 'To me, anyway. He said it was a nasty business. Dad was over there on his firm's business with his chairman the day that it happened, that's how he came to know so much about it.'

Detective Inspector Sloan got out his notebook, conscious that the connection between time and crime was a strange one. Hot pursuit always had popular support – everyone, but especially the press was usually willing to join a hue and cry. But they were less interested when this had died down. And not interested at all as the years went by – unless it was the identity of Jack the Ripper or who it was who had really killed the little princes in the Tower. 'Tell me,' he said.

'I don't know all the details,' said Marion Tridgell. 'My husband didn't like talking about it to me.'

'He did to me,' put in Paul again. 'A lot.'

'Quite so,' said Sloan, who had been taught that the exoneration of a crime didn't just come with the passage of time, old crimes being just as heinous as new ones – if not, should they have been concealed – more so. Unfortunately in the ordinary way the resolving of really old cases didn't have much support from Superintendent Leeyes, his superior officer. He didn't know yet if any of what had been said at Legate Lodge was in the ordinary way. It didn't sound like it to him. He turned to Paul Tridgell. 'This works accident in Luston, sir, what happened?'

'I can't tell you exactly,' he said, 'but someone ended up dead in a vat of chemicals or something pretty awful like that, anyway.'

'Although my husband always said it shouldn't have happened,' Marion was saying almost before her son had finished speaking.

As far as Detective Inspector Sloan was concerned that went for all accidents.

'Perhaps it was that that played on Dad's mind,' suggested Jane. 'You never know.'

'The mind's a funny thing,' agreed Detective Inspector Sloan as he and Crosby took their leave.

'Where to now, sir?' asked Crosby, clambering back into the driving seat.

'The offices of the *Luston News*, Crosby, where we are going to trace any account of an accident at the works of Luston Chemicals at an unknown date, which Derek Tridgell's son conveniently thought fit to remember to tell us about at just the right moment.'

'Yes, sir.'

'And then, Crosby, in spite of your well-known dislike of paperwork, we are going back to the police station where you are going to check on the reports of all the accidents and suicides in "F" Division.'

'How far back, sir?' He sounded glum.

'How long is a piece of string, Crosby?' He sat back in the car. 'And, Crosby...'

'Sir?'

'Check if young Master Tridgell has a record of any sort. His attitude towards the police leaves a lot to be desired.'

It wasn't until supper time at Legate Lodge that the subject of Derek Tridgell's last words came up again. Marion had spent the meal practically silent and eating very little, toying with her food all the while. Supper over, the family were all sitting round the table drinking coffee when Marion at last stirred out of the lethargy of grief and said, 'We must talk about the funeral service, Paul, now that you're back home.'

Paul Tridgell stiffened. He had made everyone in his family well aware of his disbelief in all things religious throughout his adolescence. 'Right,' he said uneasily, shooting a glance at his sister.

'The vicar's coming round in the morning to talk about the service,' his mother went on.

Paul hunched his shoulders. 'I've never understood why Dad believed in church and all that.

After all, he was a scientist.'

'He was a research chemist,' explained his mother patiently, 'and he always said that all the while he was doing inorganic chemistry he didn't believe in anything spiritual at all.'

He challenged her. 'So what made him change his mind, then?'

'When he started learning about organic chemistry,' said Marion simply. 'He said that once he got his mind round all that, his view of the world changed. Now, I've been thinking and decided that your father would have liked Simon Thornycroft to give the address.'

Paul visibly relaxed. 'Good idea, Mum. After all, he's a potholer, too.'

'He's more than that now. He's the president of the club,' said Marion, 'and I'm sure there'll be a lot of their members there.'

'Bound to be,' agreed Paul.

'All the cavers knew Dad,' said Jane, adding shakily, 'and liked him.'

'Sure,' said Paul, always faintly surprised that so many people liked the father with whom he had done nothing but argue for years.

'I'll ring Simon tomorrow and ask him if he'll do it,' said Marion, then, turning to her daughter, she asked Jane if she wanted to read something at the service.

Jane blinked. 'I don't know if I could manage it, Mum, but I think I'd like to try. There's a poem I've been wondering about.'

'And you, Paul?' Marion looked quizzically at her son. 'Are you up for it?'

'I couldn't speak about Dad, if that's what you

44

mean,' he said. 'Not in a church.'

'No,' she agreed. Since it was his frequent rows with his father that had led to Paul's nomadic existence, this did not surprise Marion. 'But you could do one of the readings if you want.'

'All right, I'll think about it,' he conceded gruffly. 'Something short, though.'

Marion sat back again and lapsed into silence.

'Come on, Mum,' cajoled Paul, newly bathed and shaved, 'cheer up. At least Dad's pain is all over now. You don't have to worry about him any more, whatever it was he said.'

His sister shivered. 'And we couldn't have told the police anything more than we did.'

'Just as well,' said Paul lightly, 'because if you hadn't I'm sure they have ways of making you talk.'

'You shouldn't joke like that, Paul,' Jane protested. 'Not at a time like this. It's not nice.'

Marion set her cup back on the table. 'Paul, I can assure you Jane and I have only told the police exactly what Daddy said that day and nothing more.'

'And how and when he said it,' added Jane, the memory of that moment still very much with her.

'Well, then what are you two worrying about?' asked Paul nonchalantly.

'It's what he said that I'm worrying about,' said Jane, exasperated. 'And why he did. Can't you understand that I'm frightened by it all?'

'That he said someone had killed a man?' Paul tilted his chair back. 'So what? They do it all the time where I've just come from. With knives, mostly.'

'Don't be silly, Paul,' said Marion calmly. 'And don't break that chair either.'

'Sorry, Mum,' he said, landing the front legs of the wooden chair back on the floor with a crash. He put his coffee cup back on the table and said, 'I must say I've had better coffee than this in Columbia.'

'Must you?' said Jane more sharply than she had intended. 'I think we should be talking about what Daddy said instead of about the quality of coffee.'

'And I think Paul is tired and jet-lagged,' said Marion with finality, 'and should go to bed now.'

Paul shrugged his shoulders. 'All right, all right, I'm just going up. But what Dad said doesn't really matter very much anyway since we don't know the identity of either the man he said who did the killing or who the unknown victim was.' He looked at his mother and sister and then asked softly, 'Or do we?'

CHAPTER FOUR

The decor of the premises of Morton and Son, funeral directors, was suitably muted when compared with that of most of the other establishments in the high street in Berebury. Even that of the frontage of the betting shop further down the road – devoted as it was to sheltering its patrons from public gaze at all costs – could not have been more discreet.

'Nothing showy at the front,' Tod Morton's great-grandfather had decreed over a century earlier and so its aspect had remained for the next fifty years. 'Put a brass plate there with the name of the firm on it and have some curtains at the back of the window,' was what he had ordained. 'And keep it private.'

It was still like that today. The bereaved could therefore slip in and out without the fear of a hard sell or being viewed from the pavement by the maudlin or curious. Actually the betting shop management went one further and, like the Royal Oak public house further along the road, had opaque glass in their windows, being more afraid of wives than of the glances of casual passers-by.

When cremations had overtaken burials in popularity, the old man's son, Tod's grandfather, had caused a tasteful rosewood urn to appear in the window as artfully placed there as any museum's objet d'art.

'And keep it private,' the next old man had added.

Tod's attempt to have flowers put there as well had been dismissed by his own father on the grounds that there were more than enough flowers about the place as it was. And that they needed attention.

'And keep it private,' his father had said.

'Tod, we would like to know when Derek Tridgell's funeral is planned,' said Detective Inspector Sloan without preamble.

'Friday afternoon,' said Tod Morton, that young sprig of the firm. He had been located by the two policemen in his shirtsleeves round the back of the building and interrupted in his daily task of washing down the firm's best limousine. He straightened up and tossed a sponge into a bucket. 'Two o'clock at St Michael's and All Angels at Friar's Flensant, should you want to know.'

'We do want to know,' said Sloan.

'And we want to be there,' added Detective Constable Crosby. This was not strictly true since Crosby didn't enjoy attending funerals any more than he liked being present at post-mortems but he knew where his duty lay.

'Something up, then?' asked Tod. 'Or shouldn't I ask?'

'Yes, there is and no, you shouldn't,' said Sloan briskly. 'What we want, Tod, is to be there as part of the crowd.'

'Not as us,' contributed Crosby.

'That shouldn't be too difficult since there will be a crowd,' forecast Tod Morton. 'Quite a popular figure in Friar's Flensant was our Derek Tridgell. And clever, too. Research chemist at work and a caver by way of recreation.' He wrinkled his nose in recollection. 'I think he used to play squash as well, one time, but you can't play that for ever.'

'Caver?'

'That's right, Inspector. One of those nutters who go down the Hoath Hole at Chislet Crags or whatever it is they call them over towards Calleford. It's on the farmer's land there and he lets them all play underground, seeing as it doesn't upset his livestock and that they do it for fun. Their idea of fun, not mine or his. At their own risk, of course.'

48

'How can you own a hole?' asked Crosby of nobody in particular.

'At least Derek Tridgell used to be a caver once upon a time,' went on Tod, ignoring this. 'I daresay he got a bit too ill for it in the end like he got too old for squash. A good player in his day, though, they said.'

'But he wasn't really all that old when he died,' said Sloan, himself a man beginning to be conscious of the passing years.

The young undertaker said judiciously, 'I wouldn't have called him exactly old myself either. Not for these days. Pancreatic cancer, I think the family said he had, poor chap. Getting more common, that is.'

That the undertaker would be more aware of current mortality trends than most people was something that hadn't occurred to Sloan before.

'They're coming in again tomorrow.' Tod Morton had long ago perfected the art of referring to the newly bereaved by the blanket term of 'the family'. Never if he could possibly help it did he ever use the word 'widow', especially when it came to heated disagreements over who wanted what at a funeral.

'And what sort of a funeral are the Tridgells having?' asked Sloan, glad that it would be a biggish one, giving all the better cover for strangers there.

'Conventional church,' said Tod promptly. 'You won't stand out in that sort of congregation, Inspector, unless you go in uniform, of course.'

'No fireworks?' said Crosby, slightly disa pointed.

'No animals, anyway, thank goodness,' said Tod. 'The last time we had a horse in the church it ate the Easter lilies. Dogs don't help, either,' he added bitterly. 'They howl. I'm sure they know who's in the coffin.'

'This funeral, Tod,' said Sloan, a busy man.

'Friday afternoon, like I said and, as far as I know, nothing out of the ordinary planned,' replied Tod. 'Service to be taken by the Vicar of Friar's Flensant, Mr Tompkinson. Nice chap with half a dozen parishes to run but a bit too keen all the same.'

Rightly taking this to mean that his homily was likely to go on too long, Sloan asked who else would be speaking.

'Couldn't say,' Tod shook his head. 'Not usually my problem, that.' When confronted by a warring family, the undertaker was actually quite skilled at steering a path between *la pompe funèbres* on the one hand and a lack of ceremony redolent of the burial of Sir John Moore at Corunna – in his cloak and without a funeral note – on the other hand. 'And it's a burial so it can take its time.'

'So all you have to do then, Tod,' observed Detective Constable Crosby, 'is to get him to the church in time.'

'You could put it like that,' said Tod seriously. 'It's the "crem" that doesn't like to be kept waiting.' He stooped to collect his bucket. 'Or as my old dad always says, it's only the deceased who's allowed to be late at a funeral. Nobody else.'

'There's something else we wanted to ask you, ͏d,' said Sloan, pulling a photocopy of a news- ͏er report out of an envelope. 'Do you remember burying a man called Michael Linane?'

'Not likely to forget it, am I?'

'Go on.'

'Nasty business.' Tod straightened up. 'When I die I want it to be quietly in a bed in my own home, not drowning in a vat of chemicals at work. And I don't want to die in hospital, either,' he added as an afterthought. 'Not these days.'

Detective Inspector Sloan was about to withdraw more press cuttings from the envelope when Tod said, 'Come inside.'

Sitting opposite the two policemen in the clients' chairs in his office, Tod studied the newspaper. "Berebury Man Killed in Works Accident at Luston",' he read aloud. 'Oh, yes, I remember that all right. Last year. Nasty business. Couldn't get it out of my mind for a bit. We buried him, seeing his being a local round here although the accident was over Luston way. We just got the remains of the poor chap afterwards. Don't always get those, of course.'

'If you don't then you can't have a funeral, can you?' remarked Crosby.

Tod looked at him curiously. 'No, you can't. It's only happened once before that I know of. Awful business, that was.'

Detective Inspector Sloan looked up. 'I don't get you, Tod.'

'There's a body down in those limestone caves that nobody could get to. We haven't buried him. Chap called Edmund Leaton, at least I think that was his name. It was a bit before my time in the firm but Dad used to talk about it. They said it was a roof fall that did that. Or was it a flash

51

flood? I don't remember now. He's still down there – been there for years. The powers that be said there was too much of a risk of another roof fall to try to get him out. The farmer hasn't let anyone down that particular cave ever since. It's out of bounds to everyone.'

Detective Constable Crosby said that he couldn't see that still being down there was any different from being buried in a churchyard since it was still earth to earth, ashes to ashes, and both churchyard and caves were underground.

'Cemeteries help the grieving process,' said Tod with assurance. 'Like that Michael Linane who got his chips last year over at Luston Chemicals. He's in the cemetery at Berebury. The family can visit his grave – they can't with the other poor fellow.'

'It wasn't a police matter, though, at the chemical works,' said Sloan. 'I've checked and, even though he lived here in Berebury, the death didn't come our way. It was all done over in Luston because that was where he died.'

'Inquest and Health and Safety Executive, if I remember rightly,' said Tod. 'I think they called it either an industrial accident or death by misadventure at the inquest. I'm not sure which. All I get after one of those is a burial order from the coroner.'

'"A rose by any other name..."' began Crosby, stopping when he realised where the quotation was going.

'Not that it matters,' intervened Tod swiftly. 'Their paperwork was perfect – the firm were very good at that – it was just the wire guard round the tank that wasn't perfect. Or rather they said that someone had pulled it back before he fell in but they didn't know who. Might even have been the deceased, of course.'

Sloan fixed Crosby with his eye and dared him to speak. This was not the moment for any discussion on whether a man had fallen or been pushed.

Or jumped.

'He had a big funeral in Berebury Parish Church,' went on Tod. 'Half of Luston Chemicals turned out for him – half of the county, too, come to that. I think the deceased was quite high up in their firm. Must have been, because there was a great tribute to him given by the chairman of his outfit. A guy called Ralph Iddon. Came in a Roller and dressed the part which always goes down well.' He winked at Crosby. 'Second-best dressed person there.'

'Who was the best dressed then?' asked the constable somewhat naively.

'The deceased, of course,' said Tod, grinning. 'Our shrouds are the best.'

'Iddon could have been feeling guilty about the accident,' said Sloan, the psychology of grief being something every policeman learnt the hard way.

'Not the man who saw him struggling in the vat, though, and said he tried to get him out,' went on Tod as if the inspector hadn't spoken. 'He wasn't at the funeral from all accounts. Notable by his absence, as they say. All too much for him, I daresay, and I don't wonder myself.'

'No,' agreed Sloan soberly, 'not the sort of

53

thing you'd forget in a hurry.'

'I daresay the dust will settle.' The young undertaker was wise before his time by virtue of his occupation. 'It usually does.'

'In time, Tod. In time,' said the detective inspector. 'Come along, Crosby. We must get going.'

It was when they were alone in the police car that Sloan sighed and said, 'We'd better look up the other death that Tod mentioned, too, Crosby. The caving one. Probably a waste of time but then,' he added resignedly, 'so much of our work is.'

'Well, Sloan?' barked Superintendent Leeyes, when the two policemen got back to the police station. 'Have you found out who killed who?'

'No, sir. Neither, sir.'

'If anyone did, of course,' he growled.

'Quite so, sir. But there was a death last year at Luston Chemicals which may or may not have been the one that the deceased had been talking about.'

'I wish you wouldn't hedge your bets all the time, Sloan,' said Leeyes irritably. 'It doesn't help.'

Detective Inspector Sloan decided against saying that false positives didn't help an investigation either and pulled out a folder instead. 'That is according to a report in the local newspaper, sir...'

'Not always the gospel truth, Sloan,' Leeyes reminded him, 'what you read in newspapers. Don't forget that.'

'No, sir,' nodded Sloan. He didn't see any point in reminding the superintendent that you didn't have to have been a policeman very long and know the inside story of what had been reported

54

to know that accuracy was not necessarily the name of the newspaper's game.

Sales were.

He cleared his throat and went on. 'According to the account in the *Luston News* that we found, sir, there was a fatality affecting a Berebury man last year in the pharmaceutical firm he worked for over in Luston that raised a few questions. It just might have been the death that Derek Tridgell talked about to his family since he was in the same line of business himself.'

'Then why weren't we told?' bounced back the superintendent, whose view of the territorial imperative encompassed all deaths in East Calleshire that weren't certified as natural – and those last preferably only so having being certified as such after a post-mortem examination by Dr Dabbe, the hospital pathologist.

'According to the newspaper report, sir, it would seem that the death was judged to be the result of an industrial accident.'

'Suspicious circumstances are always a matter for the police, Sloan,' trumpeted Leeyes. 'I don't like them being written off as accidents.'

'Yes, sir. I mean, no, sir.' He coughed and said, 'It seems that in due course the Health and Safety Executive will be bringing an action against the company – Luston Chemicals, that is – for negligence. You know, that big works on the main road from Berebury.'

'I know where it is, Sloan, thank you. A blind man couldn't miss it.'

'Sir?'

'The smell.'

'Ah, of course.'

'And the inquest verdict – as if I couldn't guess?'

'Death by misadventure.'

Leeyes sniffed.

'The coroner,' hastened on Sloan, 'was sitting with a jury, of course.' The detective inspector was conscious that red rags didn't come any redder to the superintendent – let alone a bull – than mention of the coroner. Mr Locombe-Stapleford, the current holder of that ancient office, was a long-standing arch-enemy of his superior officer.

'It appears,' resumed Sloan swiftly, 'that a man called Michael Linane slipped and fell into a vat of chemicals while at work there.'

Leeyes sat up and, less reticent than Crosby, immediately said, 'Did he fall or was he pushed?'

'According to the newspaper report of the evidence, he slipped.'

'And why wasn't the vat properly protected?'

'It was, sir, but the protective rail had been unhitched and slid back. By whom we don't yet know.'

He sniffed. 'I don't like the sound of that.'

'No, sir.' Detective Inspector Sloan didn't like the idea either of a man standing beside a vat of anything and then ending up in it. 'It wasn't altogether clear from the newspaper report why he wanted to access the vat – or even if he did.'

'Was he alive at the time?' enquired the superintendent, a policeman through and through.

Sloan reread the newspaper report and said carefully, 'There is no suggestion here that he wasn't.'

'What was in the vat?'

'The firm pleaded a certain amount of commercial sensitivity and wouldn't say exactly. They argued that as the man had drowned it wasn't...' Sloan glanced down at the newspaper report again and found the word he was looking for, 'germane.'

'A certain amount?'

'That is, they revealed some of the contents at the inquest but not all.'

'Any witnesses?'

Sloan consulted the newspaper. 'A fellow employee called Christopher Honley, their chief chemist, saw him trip but was too far away to stop him falling in and couldn't get him out afterwards. He had to shout for help but it came too late and the man drowned.'

Leeyes jerked his head. 'You'd better interview this Honley fellow.'

'Crosby's trying to find him now.'

'He's not still at the firm, then?'

'Their human resources department tell me that he took early retirement soon after the accident. They say that he was deeply affected by it but as far as they know he hasn't moved house.'

'What did the deceased do at the firm?'

'I am told, sir, that he was head of sales for their project called Mendaner.'

'And what, pray, may I ask is Mendaner?'

'The firm's patented name for the composition of one of the preparations they manufacture.' Sloan glanced down again at the newspaper report. 'I understand that it is something that works as a selective nerve regenerator after it's been damaged by illness or accident. They say it

57

helps recovery.'

'Valuable, then.'

'Very, commercially, I understand,' said Sloan, consciously splitting a hair. 'I wouldn't know about medically, sir.'

Superintendent Leeyes drummed his fingers on his desk. 'Then find out, Sloan.'

'Yes, sir.' He hesitated. 'We're also going to be looking into the record of young Paul Tridgell, the son of the man who died at Friar's Flensant saying what he did. He was in a car accident – a crash over Calleford way just before Christmas last year.' He paused and then added, 'With a fatality. Crosby turned it up in the record.'

The superintendent sniffed. 'Is that why the man ran away to South America? Couldn't live with the memory? Or because we were after him?'

'I couldn't say, sir.'

'Survivor guilt is a funny thing,' observed Leeyes.

Detective Inspector Sloan thought that remorse was a terrible thing, too, but he didn't say so.

CHAPTER FIVE

'When was it you said this road traffic accident was, Seedy?' asked Inspector Harpe. 'Last December?'

'It looks from the newspaper as if it happened sometime in the week just before Christmas,' said Detective Inspector Sloan, who had decided that

Paul Tridgell's road accident was the one line of enquiry that could be pursued from within the police station.

'There's always bad road traffic accidents round about then,' declared Inspector Harpe, Head of Traffic in 'F' Division. He was known throughout the force as 'Happy Harry' on account of his never having been seen to smile. He on his part maintained that there was never anything in Traffic Division at which to even twitch the lips. Quite the opposite, in fact. 'A fatality, did you say, Seedy?'

Inspector Harpe and his friend, Detective Inspector C. D. Sloan, were closeted in the traffic inspector's little office at Berebury Police Station. 'It looks like there was at least one dead at the time,' said Sloan. 'I don't know about later.'

'Ah, I remember that pile-up. Nasty. Proper recipe for disaster, it was.'

'Accident waiting to happen?' That was one thing to be said for the detective branch of the force: you never knew what was going to happen next. In Traffic Division you usually did.

'I'll say, Seedy. Overcrowded car, early hours of the morning, and nearly all high on drink, if not drugs. Come to think of it, though, taking drugs didn't come into that one because we checked. What they didn't take either, though, was that bend in the road outside Cullingoak. The car went straight off the tarmac and totalled into a tree. Gave us a lot of trouble afterwards, that did, seeing that the tree couldn't tell us a lot.'

'What sort of trouble?' asked Sloan curiously. He thought it was only the detective branch of the police service that encountered difficulties at work.

'Turned out to be a bit of a problem about knowing who'd been at the wheel.' He shrugged his shoulders, and went on, 'A well-meaning member of the public had come across the wreckage and sent for us and the ambulance people. But before we got there he'd got all but one of the people out – some must have been thrown out on impact – and strewn them all over the place. We couldn't work out a thing from where they were lying.'

Sloan gave a sympathetic nod. 'They say it's only a matter of time before computer generated imaging will be able to tell you where in the car everyone had been.'

'Maybe, Seedy, but in the meantime some people needed to know. The coroner, for starters.'

'Seat belts?' asked Sloan more mundanely. He didn't need telling that among those who also needed to know who had been at the wheel were the car's insurers.

'Not on your life – or, to be strictly accurate – not on their lives.' The traffic man shrugged his shoulders. 'We think a couple of them might have been thrown out of the vehicle and ended up on the actual road – the other motorist swears he didn't try to move any of them far but it didn't help. And in any case there weren't enough seat belts to go round should they have had a mind to put them on.'

'They never learn,' sighed Sloan.

'I can tell you that your Paul Tridgell – he's the one you're interested in, isn't he? – was one of the survivors in spite of roads being hard places to land on. Mind you, they had to get the fire and rescue people over there to cut one of the others out. The car was upside down which didn't help working out who had been sitting where.'

'Tridgell seems to have survived all right, physically anyway, if what I've seen of him is anything to go by,' said Sloan. There would be no real telling about the psychological after-effects of the accident without asking penetrating questions, and Sloan wasn't ready to talk to Paul Tridgell again.

Not just yet.

'You never can tell,' said Harpe lugubriously.

'So what did old Double-Barrelled make of it?'

'Locombe-Stapleford? Oh, the coroner decided that since there wasn't enough evidence to enable him to be certain who had been driving he couldn't – how did it he put it in his language? – "properly apportion culpability", especially as the owner of the car hadn't been in the vehicle. In the end he brought in a verdict of "Death by Misadventure" for the boy who was killed but he wasn't happy.'

'And even so the insurance company would still have wanted to know who had been doing the driving,' pointed out Sloan.

'And how,' said Harpe heavily. 'Not our problem, the insurance people, though. They have to fight their own corner, which I may say they usually do very well.'

'And what did the owner have to say about it? I hope the car wasn't a cut-and-shut job, or,' he added, 'taken without consent.'

'No, it was the old, old story,' said Harpe wearily. 'Boyfriend borrowed the girl's mother's car for a night out, promising to drive carefully.'

'And get the girl home by midnight, I expect,' supplemented Sloan, Cinderella not being the only one of whom this was expected. Cherished daughters came into this category, too. He homed in on the main point. 'He took the car with her mother's consent anyway, that right?'

'In the event that didn't come into it. Even that bunch of lunatics decided that the boyfriend was too drunk to drive after their evening out. They can all remember that much but they're not saying who did take the wheel. Not nohow.'

'Difficult,' agreed Sloan.

'Moreover,' snorted Inspector Harpe, 'every single one of the survivors insists that they can't remember no matter how many times we ask them.'

'It's not only the Mafia who have honour codes,' observed Sloan. 'The young have them of their own, too, as well as bad memories.'

'The boyfriend died at the scene and the daughter's been in a wheelchair ever since,' said Harpe.

'And what happened to our Paul Tridgell, then?'

'Woke up in hospital three days later and swore he couldn't remember anything at all after they left the pub. Neither, they said, could any of the others. Mind you,' he added with a cynicism borne of long experience, 'I shouldn't wonder if they'd all engaged solicitors by then. End of story.'

'Or the beginning of another one,' said Sloan

soberly, getting up to go. 'Thanks, Harry.' He paused on his way out of the traffic inspector's office. 'I suppose I'd better have the names and addresses of all the others in that car. The super's bound to ask if I've checked on them, too.'

'Be my guest,' said his friend, shoving a list in his direction.

'A nice little run for you next, Crosby,' said Detective Inspector Sloan genially after he had left Inspector Harpe's room. 'We're off to Luston. No need for speed, though,' he added, since the road between Berebury and Luston boasted the only serious stretch of dual carriageway in the county of Calleshire. He turned over a page in his notebook and read out an address there. 'I gather Acacia Avenue is in one of their leafy suburbs.'

'Didn't know they had any leafy suburbs there,' rejoined Crosby. Luston was the county's only really industrial town and was still grimy in spite of a succession of Clean Air Acts. He shrugged his shoulders and added grudgingly, 'but I suppose the nobs have to live somewhere.'

'Not only to live somewhere but like it,' pointed out Sloan, whose own mortgage for a small semi-detached house in suburban Berebury weighed heavily on the family budget at certain times of the month. 'Otherwise they move out into the countryside, double-quick.'

Where Christopher Honley lived was in a double-fronted house with garaging for two large cars. Crosby surveyed it with interest. 'Retired through ill wealth, sir, would you say?'

'It's too soon to say anything at all, Crosby,'

Sloan reproved him, 'and it's high time you learnt that.'

'Yes, sir.'

'It's a policeman's job to look and listen, not to jump to conclusions early on and don't you forget it.' Cases where the police had tailored the evidence to meld with a preconceived judgement on the guilt of the wrong person were not unknown. And not without unhappy consequences, either – for all concerned. Fitting up was what it was called in the police force and very unpopular it was with everyone outside it, especially defence counsel, the press and the Crown Prosecution Service. And their chief constable.

'Yes, sir,' said the constable, driving right up to the front door of number 24 and bringing the police car to a stop with a loud scrunch of brakes on the loose gravel.

This brought a tall, thin man to the door, a much younger man than the detective inspector had expected.

'Mr Christopher Honley?' asked Sloan.

'Yes?' responded the man warily.

Sloan flashed a warrant card and introduced himself and Crosby. 'We'd like to talk to you about the death of Michael Linane at Luston Chemicals.'

'Oh, not again,' Honley sighed. He spread his hands wide open in a gesture of despair. 'I've told everybody everything I know about a dozen times already.'

'Then,' said Crosby brightly, 'you'll have got your story off by heart now.'

'Nevertheless, Constable,' Honley turned to

him and said coldly, 'telling it again and again doesn't help in spite of what all the shrinks in the world tell you. It was all quite ghastly and I, for one, can't forget it.' Chris Honley cast them both an enigmatic look and sighed. 'I suppose you'd better come inside.'

Sitting in a comfortable chair in a well-furnished room, Sloan took in his surroundings with interest. Early retirement and unemployment had patently not yet led to any severe retrenchment on Honley's part. He must remember, though, on the other hand that it was quite possible that Crosby might have been right for once in a while and the man had retired with a handsome pay-off. For his silence, perhaps? It was impossible to say.

At this stage, anyway.

Honley said wearily, 'I just couldn't reach the poor fellow and that's all there is to it. I tried but there was nothing there for me to hang on to any more than there had been for him.' Honley sunk his head between his hands. 'Don't think I didn't try to get to him, Inspector, because I did and I've been haunted by the whole ghastly thing ever since.'

'Did you know him?' Sloan had guessed that Luston Chemicals was quite a big firm but he already knew for certain that the death of a stranger was a very different matter from the death of someone you knew. It was what made wars possible. Not murder, though. It was other things that made murder possible.

'Of course I knew him, Inspector. Michael Linane was Head of Sales here and in charge of the commercial development of one of our most successful products ever – an important job in any firm of pharmaceutical chemists.' He restated every salesman's credo. 'There'd be no use our producing something good for patients if doctors didn't prescribe it, would there?'

'None,' agreed Sloan, ignoring this piece of business thinking and cutting to the chase, so to speak. 'Tell me, what took you past this vat when you did?'

'I'd been looking out for a couple of fellows from Berebury Pharmaceuticals – they'd been over at a meeting that morning with Michael Linane and our chairman, Ralph Iddon...'

'Big job,' observed Sloan detachedly, 'being chairman of your outfit.'

'You can say that again, Inspector. But he's a very clever fellow. In his own way, that is, of course.'

'Quite,' said Sloan, wondering exactly what way that could be. It was the very clever chaps who made a speciality of doing things that were illegal who made the most trouble for the police. The unclever ones who did things that were illegal were less trouble – but then they weren't usually to be found at the head of big pharmaceutical firms.

'I can assure you that he's very good at business,' insisted Chris Honley.

Detective Inspector Sloan said he was very glad to hear it, it being always said that money made the world go round. On the other hand he wasn't sure that it made it a better place. He tucked this thought carefully away at the back of his mind against some mythical time in the future when he could consider the proposition.

'It's important in the pharmaceutical world, you know,' Honley was going on. 'Big Pharma has got very big indeed these days.'

Sloan forbore to say that in his opinion being good at one's job was important in every world.

Honley was still going on. 'Those two men from Berebury Pharmaceuticals had come over to see Michael and our chairman earlier that morning. I didn't know what it was all about at the time but there were voices raised and someone saw the men from Berebury marching out of Ralph Iddon's office looking very angry indeed. The thing was...'

'Yes?' prompted Sloan into the pause.

'Nobody knew where the pair had got to after that. They'd stormed out in such a temper and didn't wait to be steered to the front door. I happened to be passing the chairman's door at the time and was sent to help find them, and make sure that they hadn't seen anything that they shouldn't and then show them out properly.' He smiled faintly. 'You can't afford to let your business rivals loose in your works. Dangerous.'

'And did you find them?' said Sloan, making a mental note of the man's use of the word 'rivals'.

'I found one of them. Derek Tridgell – you know, the fellow who's just died. He told me that he was lost and that his boss – he's called Sharp – Jonathon Sharp – was also looking for the way out but he didn't know where he'd got to.'

'And what did your chairman have to say about that at the inquest?' asked Sloan with interest.

'That he'd had a normal meeting with the men from Berebury about the pricing of one of their

67

products, and then a short one with Michael Linane afterwards to do with increasing production of our tablet Mendaner as soon as possible. Nothing too out of the ordinary, he said, but as sales of it were taking off they had to act quickly. He said that was the last time he saw him.'

'So you gave in your notice and left your employers,' prompted Sloan, making a note. 'Why was that, then? Especially if the firm was doing so well with this product.' He glanced down at his notebook. 'Mendaner, you said it was called.'

Honley spread his hands open in a gesture of despair. 'I just couldn't go on working there, Inspector. Not without looking at the spot where poor Michael had bought it in such a terrible way every single working day. Nobody could. Oh, I know the firm was well insured and Linane's people were being looked after very well, but I found I couldn't concentrate on anything else however hard I tried. It was dreadful.'

'I quite understand,' said Detective Inspector Sloan. And he did. There were officers at the police station who couldn't ever shake off memories of tragedies they had had to attend no matter how hard they tried or for how long. Some of them retired, too, although they found out too late that even then the memories didn't go away. 'So what did you do?'

'Left the firm.' He waved a hand. 'Oh, I know it was a mad thing to do but I just couldn't stand being there any longer. Not day after day.' He looked in the direction of a side table with a studio portrait of a woman on it inside a silver frame. 'And my wife said she couldn't stand living with

68

me, being around as I was after the accident and that I had to do something about it or she would leave me. She was sure I had to leave Luston Chemicals or have a nervous breakdown – so was my doctor.'

'And so what are you doing now?' asked Sloan, there being no sign whatsoever of any downsizing about the place and sizeable cars being notably juicy.

'Nothing,' said Honley shortly. 'Well, for the time being anyway.'

'Ah,' said Sloan.

The man jerked his head. 'I suppose that you could say that theoretically I'm on gardening leave at the moment.'

Sloan raised his eyebrows. 'Only theoretically?' he queried.

'Yes, Inspector. That's all you can call it politely.'

'So you've got another job lined up,' divined Crosby.

'Will have very soon,' amended Honley. He looked at the two policemen. 'Actually, it's over at Berebury Pharmaceuticals but it doesn't start quite yet. Oh, my old firm mightn't like it but they can't stop me. My solicitors have said so. I've been headhunted, you see.'

Suddenly Detective Inspector Sloan had a burst of enlightenment and did see. 'To replace Derek Tridgell?'

'Dead man's shoes,' said Crosby complacently. 'I've heard of them.'

Honley nodded. 'That's right. And that's why I can't very well start there for a little while.'

'Not until after the man's been properly buried,'

said Crosby. 'It wouldn't be decent.'

'Their head honcho, Jonathon Sharp, is a really smart cookie, I can tell you,' said Honley.

'Sharp by name and sharp by nature?' suggested Crosby.

'He's had me lined up ever since he knew Tridgell wasn't going to get better but naturally we couldn't say anything.'

'Naturally,' agreed Sloan, making a mental note of the link between the two businesses. 'And shall you be working in the same field as Tridgell was?'

'With their product Ameliorite? Oh, no. That's all done and dusted now – it's probably not even in production over there any longer. It's dead in the water. Besides, as I said, Luston Chemicals has its own product – Mendaner – that does very nearly the same thing rather cheaper. It's up to Luston's sales team now to carry on with that. Not my pigeon, sales, thank goodness and anyway they've got a replacement for Michael lined up. No, I'll be working on something quite new that Derek had only just started out on. They'd got quite a few candidates in the pipeline over there that Derek Tridgell had been dealing with. He was a good man, you know.'

'Candidates?' asked Crosby, who had been told he wasn't candidate material for the examination for sergeant: the phrase 'In your dreams, laddy', still rankled.

'Candidates in our line,' explained Honley, 'are drugs that have been developed but not yet tested on humans.'

Crosby announced that he was against vivisection.

70

'On humans,' repeated Honley.

The detective constable raised no objection to this.

'What you do have to worry about, gentlemen, in our way of business is falling off a patent cliff.' Catching sight of Crosby's puzzled face, Chris Honley hurried to explain. 'When that happens anyone can manufacture your invention without paying you a royalty. That's why you need to have a good product line.'

'There's no sentiment in business,' remarked Crosby.

There wasn't a lot in police work either, thought Sloan, though there was often compassion, which was just as important.

'My appointment's not going to be announced until after the funeral,' Honley was going on, 'and then only after Derek's wife has been told in private.'

'Widow,' said Crosby unnecessarily.

'Which is what made your gardening leave only theoretical,' concluded Sloan, shutting his notebook. 'I understand now, sir. Thank you.'

That there was a lot more that he didn't understand, he left unsaid.

CHAPTER SIX

Of the three people standing in the hall of Legate Lodge awaiting the arrival of Derek Tridgell's cortège, his widow, Marion, was by far the most composed. She had done her grieving in private – some of it before her husband had died and some afterwards. Now she was fully in charge of her emotions and ready to deal with the demands of the funeral with dignity.

The same could not be said for her two children. Her daughter, Jane, was still visibly upset and even now unsure whether or not she could go through with the reading she had chosen. Paul Tridgell, her son, suitably dressed for a wonder, was trying to come to terms with having to play in public a role quite unfamiliar to him – that of the conventional offspring of a recently deceased parent. And in a church, at that, and in spite of proclaiming to all and sundry – including the vicar – that he didn't believe in God.

His conversion in the matter of doing a reading had come when, after thumbing through the Bible in the privacy of his bedroom, he suddenly announced that he would be doing it after all. It would be, he had said firmly, some well-known verses from the Old Testament.

By some miracle of tact the vicar had agreed, on being told this, that doing so ought not to offend Paul's principles as a non-believer. Conceding this with a gracious nod, the *enfant terrible,* who had now at last reached theoretical adolescence if not yet adulthood, assured the cleric that anyway today nobody would be in the least bit interested in what he said or did. To this the vicar had wisely made no reply.

As the hearse pulled up outside the door, Marion took a deep breath and reminded herself of one of her grandmother's aphorisms. It was important, the old lady had insisted, to be 'mistress of oneself though china fall'. As a child, Marion had never been able to decide whether she had meant china or China until it had been too late to ask her.

Both, perhaps.

Preceded by the Reverend Mr Tompkinson, Tod Morton, black top hat tucked under his arm, led the bearers and their burden up the aisle of St Michael's and All Angels at Friar's Flensant at the exact moment that the peal of muffled church bells died away. Following the coffin and rigidly looking neither to the right nor the left, it is doubtful whether Marion Tridgell registered the presence of Detective Inspector Sloan and Detective Constable Crosby in the back pew or, indeed, of anyone else at all.

Dressed as soberly as the rest of the congregation, the two policemen had stepped into the church as late as they felt they could. Not, though, as late as a very young girl who slipped into the pew beside Sloan at the very last minute. She was only seconds ahead of the arrival of the cortège and just at the moment the congregation were rising to their feet.

She whispered into Sloan's ear, 'I'm not supposed to be here. I was told not to come.'

'But you did,' he said.

'Rather. I'm not too young to come to a funeral, am I?'

The detective inspector looked down at her and said as softly as he could, 'Someone thought you were.'

'My *faux pas*.'

'Who?'

'That's what I call my stepfather. False Pa – it's rather clever, don't you think? He's not my real father, you see. I'm Lucy Leaton.'

Sloan put his finger to his lips and motioned her to be quiet as Tod Morton ushered the family to their seats and the vicar began the burial service by saying, 'We brought nothing into this world, and it is certain that we carry nothing out...'

In the rustle that followed as the congregation sat down after his opening words, the girl asked Sloan how they knew if Mr Tridgell was really in the coffin.

'We do,' he said. Surely the girl was too young to be versed in crime stories – or was it history? – where bricks had been substituted for the deceased?

'What if he's not really dead?' she asked in a hoarse whisper.

'He is,' said Sloan firmly. That was a matter for the thriller-writers whom she was much too young to have read.

'What if he knocks and wants to come out?'

'He won't,' said Sloan, this being neither the time nor the place to explain death and decay to someone who looked scarcely out of infant school. Or where the word 'wake' came from.

'Dearly beloved,' went on the vicar, 'we are gathered together today to bid our farewells to a man known and loved by us all.'

'Not everyone loved him,' hissed the small figure beside Sloan. 'They pretended to but I know they didn't.'

'How do you know?' asked Sloan as quietly as he could, and wondering if this could be important. That grist to the detective mill took many different forms was something every policeman learnt in time.

'They smiled at him too much,' she said, 'but only with their faces. Not with their eyes. He shouted at his son, too. *Faux pas* said so.'

As soon as the vicar finished his introduction the organist started to play the hymn 'The Day Thou Gavest, Lord, is Ended'. When they reached the last verse Paul Tridgell stepped out of the family pew and went to stand at the lectern. 'The reading,' he announced, 'is from Ecclesiastes, chapter three.'

Detective Inspector Sloan, well-brought-up son of a churchgoing mother, knew what was coming next and sat back.

Paul straightened the Bible in front of him and began reading.

To every thing there is a season, and a time to every purpose under the heaven;
A time to be born, and a time to die; a time to plant, and a time to pluck up that which is planted

'Why doesn't he say "harvest"?' asked the girl at Sloan's side, 'if that's what he means. Or "reap". That's what they do on farms, isn't it?'

'Be quiet,' Sloan commanded her.

Paul paused and then went on very slowly and deliberately, staring as he did so at someone unknown in the congregation, '"A time to kill..."' He looked down at the Bible and repeated, '"A time to kill, and a time to heal".'

Try as he might, Sloan couldn't make out who Paul Tridgell had been looking at so pointedly, seeing only their backs. He shot a sideways glance at Crosby sitting on his other side but that worthy, head well down, had been contemplating his shoes, clearly polished for the occasion.

Paul resumed the reading, and finished it in a level voice before making his way back to sit next to his mother in their pew. His sister, Jane, then got to her feet and, in turn, made her way to the lectern. Taking a deep breath, she began to read Christina Rossetti's poem 'Remember' that began, '"Remember me when I am gone away, Gone far away into the silent land".'

Swallowing visibly she fought back tears as she continued in a tremulous voice to read the poem to its end: '"Better by far you should forget and smile, Than that you should remember and be sad".' She walked back to the pew, eyes cast down, still patently distressed.

Towards the end of another hymn, the vicar ascended the pulpit and began his own address. He hadn't got very far into his homily before the little figure at Sloan's side bounced up and down and said, 'Boring, boring.'

'Enough,' snapped Sloan. He wanted to hear what the clergyman had to say but in the end it was nothing that told him anything more about the late Derek Tridgell than he knew already. 'People don't talk at funerals,' he whispered back, feeling a momentary pang of sympathy for whoever it was that had the misfortune of having to teach this age group. 'If you can't keep quiet you'd better go home.'

That silenced her until the vicar reached the end of his peroration with a firm assertion that 'Where there is death, there is hope' and the next speaker rose to deliver the customary tribute. Sloan glanced at the service sheet and saw that it was Simon Thornycroft, President of the Berebury Caving Club. The man was clearly a practised speaker, beginning, 'I count it a great honour and privilege to have been invited by Derek's family to pay this tribute to a very old friend, a fine man, a distinguished pharmaceutical scientist and a great caver.'

Lucy Leaton tugged at his sleeve. 'That's my *faux pas.*'

The man was still speaking. 'Jonathon Sharp, the head of Berebury Pharmaceuticals, who is present today,' here he nodded in the direction of a man sitting near the pulpit, 'has particularly asked me to tell you that without Derek's meticulous groundwork the company's important product Ameliorite would never have reached the manufacturing stage. Now it can be said that it is one of the foremost treatments in the world for damaged nerves – particularly post-herpetic neuralgia – a most painful and intractable condition.

But if anyone ever doubted how meticulous Derek was they had only to look at his perfect lawn.'

This raised a few gentle smiles all round.

The speaker changed his tone and went on more soberly, 'Nor must any of us ever forget Derek's heroic efforts to save Edmund Leaton when we were trying to explore the Baggles Bite, after that terrible accident when the roof of the cave in the Hoath Hole at Chislet Crags collapsed and the cave flooded. Derek's actions on behalf of a fellow spelunker that day went far, far beyond the call of duty.'

As Sloan made a mental note to look a new word up in his dictionary, the little figure at his side looked up at him. 'Edmund Leaton was my dad,' she said.

Detective Inspector Sloan stared down gravely at the girl, who nodded. *Faux pas* married my mother afterwards,' she said. 'I don't remember my dad. I was very little at the time.'

'Is your mother here today?'

She pointed to the back of a woman sitting near the front of the church beside the seat left empty by the speaker, auburn hair spilling out from under a little black hat. 'That's my mum.'

Detective Constable Crosby leant in front of Sloan and muttered to her in a low voice, 'And does she know you're out?'

The girl shook her head. 'Someone was looking after me but I ran away.'

'Then,' advised Crosby in a tone that Sloan hadn't heard him use before, 'if you ask me, young miss, as soon as your stepdad sits down again I think you'd better scarper. They mightn't have spotted you here.'

Perhaps, thought Sloan, Crosby was learning to be a policeman after all.

'Now hop it,' went on the constable grandly, confirming that was indeed the case.

By the time the congregation stood to sing the hymn 'Abide with Me', she had gone.

CHAPTER SEVEN

With all heads respectfully bowed as the coffin and the family left the church, it was doubtful if either Marion Tridgell or a still tearful Jane spotted Detective Inspector Sloan and Detective Constable Crosby there, both also with their heads well down. Paul Tridgell, though, did, giving them an enigmatic stare as he walked back up the aisle. Tod Morton saw them, too, but that experienced young undertaker diplomatically gave no sign of having done so.

Marion managed to maintain her poise as she shook hands with each of the mourners as they left the church and then made their way to the wake in the ancient village pub. 'How kind of you to come,' she repeated time after time, agreeing sadly with all those who said how much Derek would be missed.

'Simon,' she said, taking both of Simon Thornycroft's hands in hers as he approached. 'What you said was lovely and just right. Thank you so much.'

'It was the least I could do,' he murmured gruffly, squeezing her hands in return. 'Derek was one of the best. I thought you'd like to know that on Sunday we're going to have another go at cracking that new ghyll we've found – the one we're going to name after Derek as soon as we crack it.'

'Oh, Simon, do take care, all of you.' She shivered.

'Don't worry, Marion. Caving's a great adventure and great fun, too.'

'I was never really happy when Derek was down there.' That she wasn't ever going to have to worry about Derek ever again had not yet really dawned on Derek's widow. She looked anxiously into Simon's face. 'It's nowhere near where Edmund died, I hope.'

'No, no.' Simon Thornycroft shook his head. 'No one's been anywhere near there since the tragedy. No one at all. The farmer – old Bartlett – won't let them anyway, if he can help it, and besides you couldn't get beyond the roof fall. The Baggles Bite is underwater now anyway and the stream must have found another way out. They said all that at the inquest, remember?'

Marion nodded, becoming sadder still.

'Caving's a great adventure, Marion,' he said, 'and Derek always enjoyed it, even when...' he stopped, his voice trailing away.

'Even when things went wrong?' she said wryly.

'No, of course, not then but Ed's death was a one-off,' said Simon. 'You've got to remember that.'

'You all did what you could,' she murmured,

80

looking towards his wife, Amelia Thornycroft. 'For Amelia and little Lucy, I mean.'

'Ed was a great friend, Marion, and I still miss him,' he said earnestly.

'It's funny how having one sadness makes you think of another one,' she said, her eyes still on Simon Thornycroft's auburn-haired wife. 'At least Derek has had a proper funeral and I will have a grave to visit. It must have been an extra sadness that poor Amelia hasn't.'

Simon nodded in sympathy.

She brightened. 'But at least Amelia and Lucy have you.'

'I couldn't wish for more, even though,' he said, giving her a small smile, 'young Lucy's beginning to get a bit of a handful these days.'

She released her hands from his and shook those of Jonathon Sharp, the next in line.

'Such a great pity, Marion,' said the chairman of Berebury Pharmaceuticals. 'Derek was at the very peak of his career. We'd never ever have got Ameliorite off the drawing board without him.'

'Then let it be his memorial,' said Derek's widow. She paused and then said, 'Jonathon, Derek was very worried – until he got really ill – about what was going to happen to Ameliorite after Luston Chemicals turned so nasty.'

'He's not the only one, Marion,' he said seriously. 'We're all very worried but all we can do at this stage is wait and see.'

'That poor man who died over there...'

'Michael Linane? What about him?'

'This business of – what do you call it?'

'Predatory pricing.'

'It was all his idea, wasn't it? Derek had told me what they were going to do.'

'Undercut us by selling their Mendaner under cost until it kills off Ameliorite,' he replied, leaving unsaid the inevitable corollary, 'and us too probably.'

'How could they do something like that?'

'Easily, my dear. It's quite often done in the business world and as the health service people have to buy as cheaply as they can we don't stand a chance. Nobody's going to buy our Ameliorite now.'

'But I thought it was every bit as good as their Mendaner,' she said, patently puzzled.

'It is – it's a bit better actually, I think – but business is business,' said the chairman. 'There is one thing, though,' here Jonathon Sharp bent his head towards her and said in a low voice, 'Michael Linane was their head of sales. Now he's gone we're just waiting to see what happens next. That's all we can do.' He laid a hand on her arm. 'I'm afraid they could just be limbering up over there for an advertising campaign for their own product but don't you worry. Derek's pension's quite safe.'

Marion said perceptively, 'But you're still worried, Jonathon, aren't you?'

'Michael Linane's death might just have made them think twice,' he said, adding to himself that he didn't suppose it would.

Marion Tridgell was nobody's fool. 'Your firm's in danger, isn't it?'

She got an oblique answer. 'What we think, Marion, is that though what they're planning to do over in Luston isn't legal, there's actually not a lot we can do about it except either watch Berebury Pharmaceuticals go down the drain or come up with something as good as Ameliorite pretty quickly.'

'But if it's not legal...'

'I'm afraid that by the time we could've taken them to court the damage would have been done anyway.'

'Business is like war, isn't it?' she said, getting ready to shake the next hand in the queue in front of her.

'Just the same,' agreed the Chairman of Berebury Pharmaceuticals, 'but without the Geneva Convention.'

'I think, Crosby,' said Detective Inspector Sloan thoughtfully, as from a safe distance they watched the last of the mourners make their way from the churchyard to the Lamb and Flag Inn opposite, 'that we may now safely assume that there's been a killing.'

'And that whoever did it was in the church today,' said Crosby, cheering up.

'Probably,' said Sloan, more cautious. 'On the other hand it might just only have been Paul Tridgell's way of letting someone know that he knew something. We don't know what, I'm afraid.'

'But that's downright dangerous,' protested the constable. 'Can't he work that out?'

'I think he's probably playing with fire,' said Sloan in tacit agreement. 'You know how young men are.' He wasn't sure if Crosby actually did, he not having been a policeman all that long, so he hurried on. 'And what we need to know next is who Paul Tridgell was looking at when he repeated that bit about "a time to kill".'

'"You pays your money and you takes your choice",' quoted Crosby casually. 'Someone was at the wheel of the car that crashed. And if there was ever a really suspicious death, it was that one over at Luston.'

'Someone killed someone,' agreed Sloan, getting into the passenger seat of the police car and strapping himself in. 'We just don't know who, when and where.'

'And why,' said Crosby, starting the engine.

'Or whether it was even murder,' mused Sloan. 'People sometimes kill without having the intention of doing so. Think dangerous driving. And as it happens that could very well come into things here.'

Superintendent Leeyes sat back in his office chair half an hour later and rewarded his subordinate with a glare. 'Well, Sloan? Anything definite yet?'

As far as Detective Inspector Sloan and Detective Constable Crosby were concerned, a cup of tea at the police station canteen had had to substitute for something more traditional at the wake for Derek Tridgell in the Lamb and Flag Inn at Friar's Flensant.

'Only what you might call a straw in the wind, sir. That's all.'

'No smoke without fire, Sloan,' countered the superintendent, a man guaranteed to take an opposing view on almost any statement expressed. 'Tell me.'

'In my opinion, the son of the deceased made it

84

quite clear to someone there at the funeral that he knew something that we didn't. He definitely went in for some verbal finger-pointing but we couldn't make out who he was pointing at. Not from where we were sitting at the back of the church.'

'Pity that, Sloan.' Superintendent Leeyes gave it as his considered opinion that not knowing the whole picture was never a desirable state for the police to be in.

'Yes, indeed, sir,' agreed Sloan.

'So all you've got to go on so far is that the son – Paul, did you say his name was? – might or might not have killed someone at the wheel of a car...'

'Or known who did.'

'And a head of a sales division,' swept on Leeyes, ignoring this caveat, 'who might or might not have been pushed to his death over in his place of employment in Luston by someone whom the late Derek Tridgell knew...'

Detective Inspector Sloan wondered if Derek Tridgell himself could in all the circumstances be absolved from any crime involved but he kept that thought to himself for the time being.

'Seeing,' went on the superintendent, unaware of this thought, 'that he and his boss – what did you say his name was?'

'Jonathon Sharp,' supplied Sloan. The man was someone he had yet to talk to but he would still be at the wake now.

'Seeing,' said Leeyes, 'that they were also in the building at the time and not exactly happy bunnies from all accounts. It's not a lot to go on, Sloan.'

'There was a window of time when the two men from Berebury weren't together at Luston works and one of them is now dead.' He really would have to talk to Jonathon Sharp soon. And Ralph Iddon, too. 'But that's not quite all, sir. There's another death that keeps getting mentioned.'

'Go on.'

'There was a caving accident down the Hoath Pothole at Chislet Crags. You know, sir, where the limestone breaks out on the way to Calleford. There are a lot of caves over there.'

'Of course I know where they are,' he snapped, 'although I've never known why anyone should want to go down them.'

Detective Inspector Sloan momentarily toyed with saying that, like Mount Everest, it was because the caves were there but decided against it in the interests of his pension. Instead he said, 'I suppose, sir, you could call it mountaineering in reverse.'

'And just as dangerous,' declared Leeyes.

'So it would seem,' said Sloan. For one unknown man anyway. No, not unknown. His name had been mentioned. The late Edmund Leaton, sometime husband of Amelia Thornycroft and father of a rather precocious little girl.

'And as pointless,' said Leeyes, traversing the twelfth hole at Berebury golf course being the nearest he got to dangerous physical activity. It had a steep climb up to the tee that usually had him puffing.

Detective Inspector Sloan coughed. 'I gather the deceased, that is the late Derek Tridgell, was part of a rescue job – a failed rescue job – quite a few years ago when a man died down in a cave there.' Thinking back to the child in the church, he added, 'At least six or seven years ago if not more.'

'A crime is a crime whenever it happened,' pronounced the superintendent magisterially. 'Murder is not a price-elastic commodity.'

'Sir?'

'Potatoes aren't, strawberries are. Murder isn't.'

'Really, sir?' said Sloan, baffled.

'You don't choose whether you buy potatoes. They're a staple commodity and you need them. You only buy strawberries if the price is right and if you can afford them.'

This, decided Sloan, must be a remnant of an ill-fated course on economics that the superintendent had attended until the lecturer reached the vexed matter of the abandoning of the Gold Standard in the last Depression but one. Since anything Gold Standard being all right with the superintendent he had stalked out of the course in high dudgeon.

'I see, sir.' Sloan's own view of economics was simpler, based as it was on a combination of the parable of the six wise virgins and the six foolish ones and the dictum of a certain Mr Wilkins Micawber regarding the relationship between annual income and annual expenditure. He was unsure where murder came in. He tried again. 'About the caves...'

'I didn't like the cheese, either,' said the superintendent, a noted xenophobe, slapping his own notebook shut in the manner of one winding up an interview.

'Sir?'

'In that cave in France that I went into over there. Roquefort it was called. I prefer Cheddar. There are caves there, too, aren't there? In Somerset. English ones.'

CHAPTER EIGHT

'Where to next, sir?' asked Crosby, after they'd had the police equivalent of a funeral tea at the police station.

Judging that Jonathon Sharp might still be at the wake at the Lamb and Flag Inn at Friar's Flensant, Detective Inspector Sloan directed the constable to an address in the village of Larking instead. 'And then, Crosby, you can look up that caving accident at Chislet Crags in the *Calleshire Chronicle*.'

Crosby pulled a long face only just out of sight of the inspector.

'Police work is dull most of the time,' said Sloan, a man rather better than most at reading body language, 'and a touch too exciting when it isn't. Think Sergeant Gelven.'

Detective Sergeant Gelven of 'F' Division had made the elementary mistake of arriving too early at an armed robbery and hadn't been the same man since. And, according to the word at the station, wouldn't ever be.

Crosby steered the police car down the main street of the rural village of Larking, turning left where a poster proclaimed that the refurbished village hall was to be opened the following Saturday.

'It's that house over there, just beyond that car parked in the road,' said Sloan presently, pointing. 'The one with the little yew trees in the garden and the car outside it.'

'It's called Laguna House,' said Crosby dubiously, looking at a name board hanging outside.

'Just so,' said Sloan, leading the way up a ramp to the front door and ringing the bell but refraining from mentioning lilies.

A voice called out from inside the building. 'I'm just coming. Don't go away.'

'The police never go away,' hissed Detective Constable Crosby. 'Doesn't she know that?'

'Not yet,' said Sloan.

Eventually the door was tugged open by a young woman in a wheelchair. At the same time a youngish man slipped out from behind her and went on his way with a valedictory wave in her direction. They heard his car drive off in the road as they went into the house.

Sloan was not aware of having seen the man before but as usual made a conscious effort to remember his face. It was an automatic reaction that went with the territory, so to speak.

'Miss Elizabeth Shelford?' began Sloan.

'That's me,' she said, groaning aloud when Sloan explained that they were policemen. 'Not again! I've told everyone everything I remember about that awful accident, which is precisely nothing. I didn't remember anything at all until I came round in a London hospital about a week afterwards.' She twisted her lips into a sardonic grin. 'Unfortunately I can remember far, far too much after that. None of it good.'

Sloan asked if she was still in pain.

'Pain,' she echoed bitterly. 'Pain's the least of my problems, Inspector.' She pointed to the rug that covered her lower limbs. 'I can't feel a thing below my waist, that's the problem. Why do you think I've had those yew trees planted? Because I'm halfway to the churchyard already, that's why. Literally.'

'They should do well here,' observed Sloan, a gardener himself, thinking of the new plants rather than the thought behind them.

She gave him a bleak look. 'More than I will now, although the ground floor here's been adapted for a wreck like me. My parents have moved their sitting room upstairs to give me more space, although what I need space for these days, I'm sure I don't know.'

'Friends?' asked Sloan, interested. 'I'm sure you've still got friends except, presumably, whoever was at the wheel when you had the accident.'

'Yes, Inspector, I've still got some friends left.' Elizabeth Shelford, looking older than her years, was insistent that none of them could remember who it was who had been at the wheel of the car and they were all still friends. She tightened her lips and said listlessly, 'What does it matter now anyway? I don't know and I don't much care. My boyfriend was killed and,' she pointed to her legs, encased in the rug, 'I'll never walk again. The doctors say so.'

'Do you remember who else was in the car

when it crashed?'

'Oh, yes, that's quite different. I remember them all right. They've all been to see me since the accident except,' she said, tears welling up in her eyes, 'my Bill, of course. He only comes in my dreams.'

'And they are?' Detective Inspector Sloan had the names in his notebook but he wanted to hear her spell them out, being keen to note any inflexion or feeling that she might invest in detailing them.

'Danny Saville, Paul Tridgell, Tim Cullen, Trevor Skewis,' she said, rather as if she was reciting the song that included Uncle Tom Cobley and all, 'and,' she finished, still tearful, 'my Bill, of course.'

'Of course,' said Sloan. His friend, Inspector Harpe of Traffic Division, had handed over the results of the blood alcohol tests that had been done on all of those in the crash. It was immediately apparent that none of those in the vehicle had stuck to soft drinks that evening.

'Six in a car built for five,' observed Detective Constable Crosby censoriously.

She grimaced. 'I know, I know. We've all got to live with that but I have to exist after it, too, which is worse. At least we're all still friends and they visit me, although,' went on Elizabeth wryly, 'they don't like to come here if my mother's around. That way they think she can't blame any particular one of them. She'd like to.'

'And,' said Crosby to Sloan as the two policemen walked down the wheelchair ramp from the front door afterwards, 'it looks from what Inspector Harpe told you, sir, that if any of the others do blame one of the others, they aren't saying.'

'We'll see about that,' said Sloan, almost to himself. Raising his voice a little, he said, 'We'll try Danny Saville next in the high street in Almstone first, since we're out in the sticks already and he was in the car that crashed. It's not far from here.'

'I was so wasted I fell soft,' said the young man who came to the door in answer to their knock. He was still limping quite badly. 'Not soft enough to save me from this, though.' He pointed to his left leg. 'A comminuted fracture, they called it at the hospital.' He shivered visibly at the memory. 'Broken bones sticking through the skin and all that.'

'So you can't remember who was driving?' said Crosby, quite forgetting all he had been taught about not asking leading questions.

'I had the father and mother of a bump on my head – it came up like a chicken's egg,' said Danny Saville, 'and I can't remember anything at all except the noise of the air ambulance. Then I blacked out. Next thing I remember is coming round in the hospital in Calleford with a hell of a pain in my leg. They tell me there's a load of titanium in it now, keeping it all together.'

'I see,' said Detective Inspector Sloan and thereafter maintained a stony silence.

'All I can tell you,' said Saville presently, provoked into speech by this well-known police technique of saying nothing, 'is that it wasn't Elizabeth's squeeze, Bill. He was so blathered that the others wouldn't let him get near the wheel. He could hardly stand, let alone drive. No head for drink, I suppose.' Danny Saville said this in a tone of one sympathising with a congenital infirmity.

'Or too much drink taken,' suggested Sloan, using an old-fashioned phrase he had heard his mother use.

'They were just having a Saturday night out,' protested Saville sadly.

'Didn't you have a designated driver?' asked Crosby, a man well used to nursing the statutory orange juice while his own mates enjoyed themselves.

The young man shook his head. 'Afraid not. I didn't even know the others all that well then. I'd just hitched a lift with them because they were coming out this way. Saved me the cost of a taxi fare.' He twisted his lips. 'They told me at the hospital that it nearly cost me a leg.'

'Not an arm and a leg,' said Crosby wittily.

The man gave him a considering look and then said, shuddering, 'It was a very nasty crash. We've all had a dose of survivor guilt because of Bill dying and what happened to poor Elizabeth – that's what they call it, isn't it? Survivor guilt?'

Detective Inspector Sloan nodded. They met quite a lot of that in police work too: especially parents who thought they should have died and not their children. People who escaped disasters that engulfed their friends were another large group. His thoughts strayed to the death in the caves – perhaps those who had survived that suffered from survivor guilt, too. Perhaps he should find out.

Danny Saville was still talking. 'It seems that Paul Tridgell had it the worst. Because of Bill dying, of course. He couldn't bear to visit Elizabeth to begin with and then he decided it might help to go away for a while. He's back at Friar's Flensant again, though, because of his father dying. Actually,' he glanced at the clock on the mantelpiece and said, 'he must be at the funeral there just about now. The other two were going to go to it, too. They were Paul's best mates, you see.'

'Were they, indeed?' said Sloan, making a mental note – this time of the names of Trevor Skewis and Tim Cullen before they left.

'Just a few questions, Doctor, if we may,' said Detective Inspector Sloan, plumping himself down in the chair usually occupied by the patient, whilst Crosby took a back seat and settled down on the one meant for the patient's friend. 'About a patient of yours – a deceased patient.'

Sloan had entered the general practitioner's consulting room with a certain unworthy feeling of satisfaction, irrationally pleased at having defeated the spirited attempts of the receptionist to defend her employer from any extra intrusion on his time. The inspector had turned down her offer of an appointment later with a sad shake of his head. The doctor's patients might have to wait days for one such but not policemen on duty.

Dr Angus Browne looked interrogatively at the two policemen. 'Who?'

'Derek Tridgell at Friar's Flensant.'

'What about him?'

'How mentally competent was he?'

'I would have said that until the painkillers really took hold he knew what was going on.' He looked enquiringly at the two policemen. 'Why?'

'His wife has told us that he became very voluble as time went on,' said Sloan.

'That's true.' Dr Browne nodded. 'He was usually rather a reserved man, you know, but he started babbling a bit once he was on the stronger analgesics.' He pushed a stethoscope to one side and said, 'I'm afraid that there wasn't an awful lot I could do for him by that stage except keep the pain down and control any vomiting. Why do you ask?'

'We have been told that he is said to have made certain allegations just before he died,' said Sloan, 'and we have a duty to investigate them.'

The two bushy eyebrows on the doctor's face were raised alarmingly. 'About his care?' he asked.

'No, no,' said Sloan hastily. 'I understand the family are very happy with all the treatment your patient received.'

The eyebrows sank back to their normal position on the doctor's countenance. 'So?'

'We would like to know if he could have been hallucinating towards the end of his life.'

'Oh, yes,' said Dr Browne. 'Easily.' He cast a shrewd look in Sloan's direction and added, 'But I don't think he was.'

'Why do you say that, Doctor?'

'Because he was lucid and making sense until not very long before he died.' The general practitioner sat back in his chair. 'Remember that a dying man is rather like a guttering candle – moments of flickering darkness and then every now and then a sudden flaring of light.'

Detective Inspector Sloan nodded his understanding of this. It was, of course, just that Derek Tridgell's sudden flaring of light had led to complications, although he did not say so.

'And sometimes,' went on the doctor in a hortatory manner, 'the patient is aware of *angor animi...*'

Reminding himself that speaking in tongues – especially Latin ones – went with medical practice, Sloan deliberately raised his own eyebrows.

Dr Browne readily translated. 'It's the sense of being in the act of dying, Inspector, which I may say is not the same as the fear of death or the desire for death.'

All Sloan could think of was what a counsel – defence or prosecution – could make of this.

A great deal.

'Besides,' went on the doctor, 'the patient was a very rational man – a good scientist – before he became ill. In fact, I understand he was instrumental in bringing an important new product called Ameliorite to the market for his firm.'

'Go on,' said Sloan. 'I'd like to know about that.'

'Something much needed to assist nerve regeneration. It was good stuff.' He sighed. 'Even so, we're encouraged not to prescribe it any more, more's the pity.'

'Too dangerous?' suggested Sloan, the consequences of the drug thalidomide having cast a long shadow. After hearing Chris Honley's account, Sloan wanted to hear from a medical professional that it was unsafe.

Dr Browne shook his head. 'No, it's because there's a much cheaper product on the market these days which we have to use instead.'

'Called Mendaner?' hazarded Sloan.

'That's the one, Inspector. It does much the same job as the other, of course, but neither of them would have done this patient any good unfortunately.'

'Did Derek Tridgell know he was going to die?'

'Oh, yes, Inspector,' said the general practitioner briefly. 'He asked me and I told him. And his wife. They were too old and aware for me to try to steal death.'

'Steal death?' queried Sloan. He thought he knew the Theft Act backwards and he couldn't remember death coming into that.

'Making sure that the patient dies without knowing that he or she is dying,' said the doctor. 'It's not so popular these days. Everyone seems to be told now.'

'Whether they like it or not,' concluded Sloan quietly.

'The longer you live, the sooner you'll die,' remarked Detective Constable Crosby to nobody in particular from the sidelines.

'I was taught, Inspector, that a good physician appreciates the difference between postponing death and prolonging the act of dying. And about *ars moriendi*.'

'What's that?' asked Crosby.

'Dying well,' said the doctor pithily.

'And would what he said when he was dying have been affected by the drugs he was on?' asked Sloan, first and foremost an investigating officer.

'Everything he said and did would have been affected by them,' said Dr Browne unequivocally.

'We're not talking aspirin here, Inspector. More the double effect.'

'The double effect, Doctor?' What Detective Inspector Sloan was wondering was whether, although they might not be talking aspirin, they might be talking involuntary euthanasia instead: a mercy killing by another name, perhaps?

'The double effect is dealing with pain at the expense of shortening life,' said the doctor concisely.

Detective Inspector Sloan decided that though he might not have known what the double effect was, he did recognise hair-splitting when he met it.

The general practitioner could have read his mind because he said, 'That, for your information, Inspector, is not the same thing as a mercy killing.'

Detective Constable Crosby, his wayward interest suddenly engaged, leant forward and asked, 'What is it, then?'

'A factor in the age-old struggle between pain and death, Constable,' said Dr Browne. 'I don't know about you, gentlemen, but I myself think it better that death wins.'

CHAPTER NINE

'Mind if I go out tonight, Mum?' asked Paul Tridgell, reappearing downstairs from his bedroom dressed in his usual relaxed gear again. His dark suit had already been consigned to the back of his wardrobe.

All three members of the bereaved family were back again at Legate Lodge in Friar's Flensant after the funeral. Metaphorically as well as literally, shoes were being kicked off.

'Of course not, dear,' said Marion Tridgell.

Jane said quickly, 'I'm staying in with you, Mum.'

'That will be nice, dear,' her mother said placidly. 'Thank you.'

'Don't cook for me tonight,' said her son, making for the door. 'I couldn't eat another thing.'

'Me neither,' chimed in Jane.

'I thought the Lamb and Flag did everything very nicely today,' murmured Marion absently. 'Everyone said so. I must remember to thank them tomorrow.'

'I thought,' went on Paul, 'that I'd just pop over and have a word with Elizabeth. Let her know that I'm safely back and all that.'

'That poor girl,' said Marion compassionately.

'And catch up on things,' he said vaguely.

'Your friends Trevor and Tim came to the funeral,' said Jane. 'I saw them there.'

'So did I,' said her brother shortly.

'I didn't really see anyone at all in the church,' confessed their mother. 'I couldn't help just looking at the coffin all the time and thinking of your poor father lying there in it.'

Paul, embarrassed, paused with his hand on the door handle. 'There's just one thing, Mum...'

'What is it?'

'Dad's caving stuff. You haven't given any of it away, have you?'

'No,' she said, shaking her head. 'It's all at the back of the garage. I haven't touched it. I couldn't bear to, not after ... when...' her voice trailed away into silence.

'Right,' he said.

She swallowed. 'It's exactly where he left it the last time he came back from the Crags. He was looking like death and said he couldn't go back down there again no matter what.' Marion Tridgell's hard-won reserve started to crumble. 'He told me that he'd been back to Hoath Hole to say goodbye to Edmund Leaton.' She brushed a little tear away from the corner of her eye.

Paul stiffened. 'Dad said what?'

'Well, your father knew he was going downhill quite fast. You should have seen him, Paul. He looked quite terrible and he was losing weight by the week. He'd lost all his strength, you see, and he didn't think he could climb out of there ever again.'

Jane's head came up. 'But I thought the farmer had said no one was to go down there ever again after the roof fall.'

Marion looked confused. 'Perhaps he had but

your father got in all right. He mustn't have asked old Bartlett – he's the farmer over there – and the man couldn't be everywhere on the farm.' A faint smile crossed her lips. 'Bartlett might even have been at Berebury Market that day – your father wasn't silly, you know.'

'Dad always told me that the whole place is riddled with caves that lead one into the other,' said Paul. 'I knew that anyway. Don't you remember Dad took me down there once and tried to get me to crawl along a streamway. Hoped I'd take up caving like him, I expect.' He shuddered. 'Fat chance. Give me the open air any day.'

'And fast cars,' said his sister.

'That's unfair, Jane, and you know it.'

'All right, then. Snorkelling, not fast cars. Anyway, I thought you didn't like potholing. You always said so. So why do you want Dad's gear now?'

'Be quiet, both of you,' snapped Marion, unexpectedly fierce. 'I won't have you two quarrelling today of all days.'

'Just letting off steam, Mum, that's all,' said Paul cheerfully, slipping out of the door as he did so. 'Put it down to sibling rivalry.'

'It's been a long day,' said Marion when he'd gone. She sank back thankfully into a chair. 'And Jane...'

'Yes, Mum?'

'If the phone rings, don't answer it.'

'No? Why not?'

'If,' said her mother shakily, 'I have to tell one more person that I'm quite all right, thank you, I'll tell them what it's really like to watch someone you've loved die like your father did after twenty-five years of happy marriage and after the funeral come back to an empty house, I'll scream.'

Jane, dismayed, said, 'But you've still got us.'

'I'm sorry, dear.' Her mother pulled herself together with a visible effort. 'Of course I have. But you know what I mean.'

Jane Tridgell, maturing by the minute, wasn't sure that she did.

Detective Inspector Sloan, sitting beside Crosby who was at the wheel of the police car, directed the constable towards one of Berebury's best residential areas. Beginning its life as a country market town, there had been a gradual accretion over the years of good houses on its fringes. As agricultural prosperity had waxed and the railway arrived in the town, other businesses had come there and now it was a flourishing settlement in the heart of rural Calleshire.

Jonathon Sharp lived in one of the very best of the good houses. Double-fronted and built along the plain but ample lines that betokened a good architect, there was a deceptive simplicity about its appearance. As they approached, Detective Inspector Sloan noted with approval the detail of what was called door furniture – an elegant letter box, a finely worked key escutcheon and a substantial ornamental door knocker. He applied his hand to this, confident that the powerful car in the drive marked the return of its owner from the wake at the Lamb and Flag Inn at Friar's Flensant.

The woman who answered his knock on the door invited them in and said that her husband was just changing and would be down in a minute. As she led the way indoors, Jonathon Sharp came down the stairs in an open-necked shirt and trousers that Sloan categorised as recreational, even though he himself put on much less elegant wear for his own recreation of gardening. Sharp was a big man, with broad shoulders, but far from flabby. Sloan would not have been surprised to learn that rugby had been his choice of sport.

Unlike most people, Jonathon Sharp did not immediately overreact to the mention of the word 'Police'. Instead, he waited in a controlled manner and then asked courteously, 'In what connection?'

'A death at Luston Chemicals,' said Sloan.

Jonathon Sharp's shoulders sagged. 'That poor man...'

'Michael Linane,' said Crosby.

Sharp ran a hand through his hair and said, 'I didn't actually see him afterwards, thank God, but I gather it was all pretty terrible.'

'Terrible but not pretty,' offered Crosby from the sidelines.

'But you did see him before?' persisted Sloan.

'Of course, Inspector. We – that is my chief scientist, Derek Tridgell and I – had gone over to Luston earlier that day expressly to see him and my opposite number there, their chairman Ralph Iddon.'

'And why was that, sir?' Asking questions to which they already knew the answers was a police technique learnt early on. If nothing else, it was a test of accuracy.

Or memory.

Or something else: those who remembered a day too well could be suspect if they couldn't remember the days either side of it equally well. That could betoken a memory too well rehearsed.

'To see if we could come to some agreement about the marketing of our respective products, Inspector,' went on the man, unaware of Sloan's train of thought. 'The two have similar clinical outcomes even though they are very different pharmacologically.'

'But patented?'

'Oh, yes,' said Sharp wearily. 'You could say that the patents were the least of our problems.'

'And you couldn't come to any agreement?'

'That, Inspector, would be putting it mildly. Ralph Iddon, their chairman, and his head of sales, Michael Linane, wouldn't even countenance discussing the matter.' He gave a bitter smile. 'They were hell-bent on destroying us and it looks as if they will do just that before too long.'

'Taking you to the cleaners, are they?' asked Crosby chattily.

'Trying to,' growled Sharp. 'All we can do now is to try to come up with something else new.'

'And different,' chipped in Crosby.

Jonathon Sharp stared at him. 'Naturally, Constable. Let me tell you that Berebury Pharmaceuticals most certainly isn't into manufacturing "me, too" drugs.'

'And what might they be, sir?' asked Sloan. He wasn't sure whether he was taking a crash course in business at its worst or in the drug industry

104

behaving badly.

'"Me, too" drugs, Inspector,' explained Sharp, 'are ones made by other manufacturers climbing on the bandwagon after someone else – such as our firm – has done all the hard work of research and initial marketing.'

'The easy way,' remarked Crosby at Sloan's elbow.

'I see, sir,' said Sloan, ignoring this. 'So you and your chief chemist…'

'The late Derek Tridgell,' said Sharp. 'The man's died, more's the pity. We're missing him a lot.'

'So you and he,' went on Sloan, undeflected by this, 'went over to Luston Chemicals hoping to make them change their minds? That it?'

'Well, try to reach a compromise, perhaps.'

'You were in the last-chance saloon anyway, weren't you?' remarked Crosby unnecessarily.

'It was worth a shot,' said Sharp, looking curiously at the constable. 'Not that it got us anywhere. Ralph Iddon – I think I told you he's their chairman – was backing his head of sales all the way.'

'With pound signs in his eyes,' added Crosby for good measure.

'The first duty of a company is to its shareholders,' intoned Sharp. 'Like it or not, gentlemen, that's the law of the land. In the last analysis I suppose we could go in for manufacturing generic drugs if we wanted to do so but it's not the same.'

Detective Inspector Sloan's head came up like a gun-dog pointing. 'Generic drugs?' He'd never come across anyone pushing those. Heroin and cannabis, yes, in plenty but not generic ones.

'Out of patent products,' amplified Sharp. 'Anyone can manufacture them. The National Health Service likes them because they're cheaper.'

'But not better?'

'They are said to be the same, Inspector,' said Sharp.

'If you believe that, you can believe anything,' muttered Crosby, sotto voce.

'But the patients don't always think so,' Sharp went on, choosing not to hear this.

'But you don't make them?' asked Sloan.

'We prefer to stay at the cutting edge of research,' said Sharp austerely.

'Even though it's a dangerous place to be?' asked Sloan. They knew all about the other sort of cutting edges at the police station. 'Bladed items' was what they called them when giving evidence in assault cases.

They were very dangerous, too.

Jonathon Sharp shrugged shoulders that would have sat very well on a prop forward. 'Some you win, some you lose.'

'And have you lost?' enquired Crosby with interest.

'Not yet,' said Sharp grimly. 'And not, gentlemen, if Chris Honley and I can help it.' He waved an arm. 'He's the new man I've got coming into the firm to take Derek Tridgell's place.'

'Now that Derek Tridgell is dead,' observed Crosby unnecessarily.

'I shall be seeing Marion Tridgell this week and telling her what's happening,' said Sharp stiffly. 'She'll understand, gentlemen. Corporate wives do.'

The image of Sloan's own wife, Margaret, floated into his mind. Policemen's wives had to understand a lot, too. Their husbands coming home desperately late or working all the hours that God gave were the least of them. Husbands coming home dead-tired happened, too, but worst of all was husbands coming home emotionally drained to the dregs of their beings and not being able to say why. Sympathy had to be wordlessly implied, restlessness during the night ignored and long silences forgiven until a man had thawed out emotionally, so to speak, and was ready to resume normal life.

'This man Chris Honley is the white hope of the side, is he?' asked Crosby.

Sloan made a mental note to discuss with the constable the inappropriateness of colloquial speech during an interview just as soon as they got back to the police station.

Sharp gave him a twisted grin. 'You could put it like that, Constable. Actually Chris is taking up our Project 242 where Derek Tridgell left off. What we hope,' he said, confirming Sloan's guess that he was a rugby player, 'is that he'll pick up the ball and run with it.'

CHAPTER TEN

'You've got to hand it to him, sir,' remarked Crosby as the two policemen left the house and walked back to the police car. 'If you ask me, he's pretty smart.'

'He doesn't hang about,' conceded Detective Inspector Sloan. He reluctantly admitted, too, to the constable that they had been very little wiser at the end of the interview than they had been at the beginning. He agreed, though, that the chairman of Berebury Pharmaceuticals was playing at the sharp end of the keyboard. Even to not telling the police that the aforementioned Chris Honley was coming to the firm from that of their deadly enemy, Luston Chemicals.

'But we knew that anyway,' protested Crosby.

'That's not the same thing at all,' said Sloan.

Crosby, who wasn't sure what he had meant by this, aimed a kick at the front tyre of the police car. 'Where to now, sir?' he asked instead.

'Back to base,' said Sloan, adding simply, 'if not square one.'

He didn't know whether the dice were loaded against the police or if this was just the feeling he usually had during a case. He didn't even know for certain, at this stage, what sort of a case the police had. The only thing he was sure about was that two intangibles – a deathbed statement and a young man staring meaningfully into a congregation when giving a biblical reading that mentioned a killing – hardly amounted to evidence of the level required by the Crown Prosecution Service.

Detective Constable Crosby had his mind on other things. 'Isn't it a crime to poach someone else's employee, sir?'

'You'll have to look that one up,' said Sloan absently. What with golden hellos and golden handcuffs, he wasn't at all sure about employment laws any more. And you didn't go on gardening leave when you left the police force. You just went in search of another job to keep the home fires burning.

The game of snakes and ladders still on his mind as they travelled back to base, Sloan was beginning to think that they might need to throw a six to begin on this case. He was not yet sure either whether there were any snakes on the board in the shape of murderers, or ladders in the form of evidence.

What was waiting for them back at the police station could have been either.

Or both.

Or neither.

Sitting on his desk was a wodge of photocopies of press cuttings from the Calleford weekly local paper, the *Calleshire Chronicle*.

'They're about that caving accident, sir,' said Crosby, laying them out in front of the inspector. 'The one over at Chislet Crags.'

'The third man,' said Sloan enigmatically, conscious that he would have to be careful not to get carried away in the matter of deaths like the man, given a hammer, who saw nails wherever he looked. 'Well, it's the third death that we know about, anyway.'

'It looks as if there were actually four of them there, sir,' the constable said stolidly. 'It says here that the party was led by Edmund Leaton, who was followed by Simon Thornycroft, Derek Tridgell and a Katherine Booth, whoever she might have been.'

Sloan pulled the papers towards him and read a headline aloud. 'Tragedy Underground at Chislet Crags. Death in the Caves.' Automatically he glanced at the date of the newspaper. 'Let me see, it's five – no, six – years ago now.'

'Long enough for the dust to have settled,' said Crosby, who was still young enough for six years to seem an aeon of time.

'Time for a lot of things,' growled Sloan, 'but, according to Tod Morton at the undertakers, not long enough to have got the body out.'

'If they tried,' pointed out Crosby.

Sloan scanned the text. 'It looks as if the others there tried to do so all right at first but that a lot of water started to build up in front of the rock-fall because the stream was blocked and they had to get out pretty quickly. It says here that the cavers went down again later with police divers but even so they didn't get very far.'

'Nasty,' observed the constable.

'And,' said Sloan, still reading aloud, 'since they didn't know how long the rockfall went on for or how dangerous it would be to try to shift the debris, especially underwater, it looks as if they...'

'Trod water?' suggested Crosby.

'Were afraid of setting off another roof fall,' said Sloan coldly.

'They manage to do it in coal mines,' said Crosby. 'What's the difference?'

'Health and safety,' said Sloan.

'How did they know he, whoever he was...?'

Sloan interrupted him. 'We know who he was, Crosby, remember. He was the father of that chatty child who sat next to us in the church and he was mentioned at the funeral service, too.' He searched his memory for a name. 'Leaton, that was it. Besides, his name is here in the paper: "Edmund Leaton, a married man with one child".'

'How did they know he hadn't escaped and was waiting for rescue on the other side of the rockfall, sir?'

Detective Inspector Sloan bent his head over the press cuttings again. It took him a minute or two to find the answer to that. 'It seems that they were all pretty sure that the rockfall had killed him. It was a big one. Besides, they didn't know if there was another side of the Bite that they could get to. That was the trouble. It seems that finding that out was the object of the exercise that day – to see if there was anything in the way of a new cave beyond what they called the Baggles Bite.' He paused and said pensively, 'If there was, they didn't reach it.'

'Some people get their pleasure in funny ways,' said Crosby. 'That reminds me, sir, have you heard about the man who practised animal husbandry until the police found out and arrested him?'

'Yes,' said Sloan briefly. 'A very long time ago.'

He scooped up the press cuttings. 'Find out where this Katherine Booth and Simon Thornycroft live while I talk to the superintendent.'

Superintendent Leeyes listened carefully to Sloan's account of the chairman of Berebury Pharmaceuticals, Jonathon Sharp's, hiring of Chris Honley from their business rivals, Luston Chemicals.

'Even before his friend Derek Tridgell had died, you say?' said Leeyes, unusually wide-eyed. 'What sort of a school did the man go to, one where they hit men when they were down?'

'I couldn't say, I'm sure, sir,' said Detective Inspector Sloan, alumnus of St Martin's Primary and Berebury Grammar Schools. He knew, though, that all schoolboys had a code of honour, and one which he didn't think would have included filling a friend's position at work while he was still dying. Not unless it was really urgent.

'I don't like the sound of that, Sloan.' The name of the superintendent's old school was not known to his underlings, although Borstal and sundry other young offenders establishments were often suggested.

'No, sir.'

'Not cricket.'

'Definitely not, sir,' said Detective Inspector Sloan, whose own ethics came from an amalgam of the Ten Commandments, the Scout Law and *Stone's Justices' Manual.*

'Doesn't seem right to me, all the same,' sniffed Leeyes.

'No, sir, me neither,' agreed Sloan, who knew all about honour among thieves but not a lot

112

about ethics in other fields.

'Jonathon Sharp could have had a lot to gain by that fellow who fell into a vat and died, couldn't he?' mused Leeyes. 'And probably has by his poaching of Chris Honley, too.'

'It would seem so, sir,' said Sloan, 'but Ralph Iddon, Luston Chemicals' chairman, could still carry on with his war of attrition without both of them and no doubt will.' He toyed with the idea of saying something about the waters closing over a man's head when he wasn't there, but discarded it as inappropriate in the sad circumstances of the head of sales at Luston Chemicals' terrible death in a vat of chemicals.

'And,' went on Leeyes, 'you say this Jonathon Sharp was in the building at the time, pleading for mercy...'

'Or words to that effect,' put in Sloan, who didn't know exactly how the chairman of Berebury Pharmaceuticals had made out his case for peaceful coexistence. Perhaps there was no such thing in business.

As there wasn't in some warring cultures.

'And you say that Derek Tridgell – the late Derek Tridgell – was there in the building, too, at the same time.'

'Yes, sir.'

'And he's the man who had insisted that there had been a murder.'

'Yes, sir.'

'Was this Jonathon Sharp at the funeral, too?'

'Yes, sir. I know that because his name was mentioned.' Sloan indicated a file in his hand. 'He wasn't down in that cave, though, where another man was killed.'

'He probably had more sense than to go caving,' said Leeyes robustly. 'He sounds a very clever fellow to me.'

Marion and Paul Tridgell were both at home the next morning when Jonathon Sharp called at Legate Lodge. Jane had gone out.

'I hope I haven't come at an awkward time,' Sharp began as he accepted Marion's warm invitation to come in and sit down.

'There's always a bit of a lull after a funeral,' Marion said obliquely.

Paul muttered only just out of the visitor's hearing, 'After the Lord Mayor's Show, comes the dustcart.' His mother heard him, though, and frowned, shaking her head at her son.

'I needed to see you, Marion,' said Sharp gruffly, ignoring Paul. 'It's about the legacy of Derek's work, his good work. His very good work.'

'It was,' she said, nodding. 'I do know that. I always have.'

'And I know it's a cliché but life does go on,' said the chairman, unusually tentative.

She sighed. 'I know that, too, Jonathon, only too well.'

'Marion, I am sure that we can't ever really fill Derek's place ... he was truly a key man at Berebury Pharmaceuticals...'

Paul erupted from the other side of the room. 'But you're going to have a damn good try, aren't you?'

'Your father is irreplaceable,' said Sharp, turning to him, 'but the business has to go on too. We

114

all depend on it.'

'Capitalist!'

'Paul,' protested Marion, 'your father would have understood what Jonathon is saying.'

Paul looked at the chairman angrily. 'You've got someone lined up to fill his shoes, haven't you? I bet you've had him in your sights for ages – even while Dad was dying. Must have, if you're talking about taking him on already.'

Jonathon Sharp had the grace to look uncomfortable. 'It was important that we went for the right person.'

'I'll bet,' said Paul derisively. 'I've heard all about the funeral baked meats coldly furnishing forth the marriage tables, too. It's in *Hamlet* if you haven't come across it.'

'I know, Jonathon,' intervened Marion quietly, 'that you'll need a very special person to fill Derek's shoes.'

'That's exactly who we've gone for,' said Sharp.

'Well, then, who is it?' demanded Paul. 'Someone that Dad would have known and hated?'

'Known but not hated,' protested Sharp. 'There aren't all that many men in his particular speciality and in the nature of things they mostly get to know each other.'

'What does that mean?' asked a truculent Paul.

'As I said, it means that it was important that we went for the right person. We couldn't afford any delay either.' Sharp looked from mother to son. 'Pharmaceuticals is an industry that doesn't sleep.'

'And of course money doesn't have feelings,' said the young man. 'And that never sleeps either.'

'It's not that,' said Sharp uneasily.

'Well?' Paul demanded. 'What is it, then?'

'I wanted your mother to know before I announced it, that's all.'

'All right, then. Tell us. Who is it?'

'Chris Honley.'

'Never heard of him,' declared Paul.

'Chris Honley from Luston Chemicals?' asked Marion, who obviously had.

Jonathon Sharp nodded. 'Their bright boy.'

'Oh, no,' Paul howled. 'I don't believe it! How could you? Sleeping with the enemy. That's what I call that.'

CHAPTER ELEVEN

Detective Inspector Sloan's first action on getting to the police station the next morning had been to ring his friend, Harry Harpe of traffic division.

'Harry,' he said, 'there was something I forgot to ask you to spell out for me about that road traffic accident I got you to look up.'

'Go ahead.'

'You remember, don't you, it was the one with the Tridgell son involved.'

'What about it?'

'All those youngsters in the car swore that they didn't know who was driving when they crashed—'

'They did know all right but they clammed up,'

interrupted Harpe. 'I'm pretty sure about that and anyway you can usually tell.'

'That's what I mean. Why did they gang up like they did? Remind me exactly what did they have to gain by us or anyone else not knowing who it was?'

'Up to fourteen years of freedom for one of them, the one who was driving, that is,' said the traffic inspector promptly. 'In other words, Seedy, not going to prison for a maximum of fourteen years on a charge of causing death by dangerous driving. Plus an obligatory driving ban for two years and an unlimited fine. If proved in court,' he added from sheer force of habit. 'Mitigating circumstances come into it, of course, but that's for the court. They don't ask me.'

'Fourteen years is a long time,' reflected Sloan.

'If you ask me it should be life, not fourteen years,' growled Inspector Harpe, a man who had had perforce to attend every road traffic accident in East Calleshire for years and years. 'Especially as they were all under the influence. You get up to fourteen years for causing death by careless driving under the influence of drink, too,' he growled, 'in case anyone thought the lesser charge would be better for the accused.'

Lesser charges were never the flavour of the month with the traffic inspector. Or with Superintendent Leeyes. Detective Inspector Sloan was more pragmatic, feeling as he did that circumstances altered cases – even police ones.

'And they were all friends, except one of them,' said Sloan, remembering that that particular man, Danny Saville, had not been at Derek

117

Tridgell's funeral with the others. He was the one who'd only accepted a lift that night. Even so he, too, had remained silent on the matter of who had been at the wheel.

'And an obligatory driving ban for at least two years plus a compulsory driving retest does make a driver think,' completed Harry Harpe with a certain amount of relish.

The pony club's mantra that if you fell off a horse you were supposed to get straight back into the saddle again before fear could set in obviously didn't apply to dangerous drivers. They had to come to terms with driving again two years after a fatal accident: not easy, thought the detective inspector who had not so far ever sat astride a horse.

Sloan swiftly changed tack before the traffic inspector could progress to hanging, drawing and quartering. 'Tell me, Harry, what hope do you still have of finding out which of them was driving?'

'Not a lot,' replied Harpe gloomily. 'Not short of finding fingerprints on the steering wheel or the gear lever which I may say we couldn't, or DNA on the driving seat which had been covered in oil so we couldn't do that either.'

'DNA anywhere else?' asked Sloan. 'I mean then you might have been able to place one or other of them in the back.'

'No such luck. Without seat belts, they'd all been tossed about so much inside the vehicle that we couldn't make out which of them had been sitting where.' He sighed. 'I assure you, Seedy, that it's not for want of trying that we couldn't nail the driver. The others – the passengers –

don't come into it, of course. Not in our book.'

'No, no,' said Sloan hastily, 'I know that.' Meticulousness figured high in the traffic inspector's code.

'As far as I can see,' said Harpe, 'there're only two ways that we're ever going to get whoever was at the wheel of that car into court. Either an accusation by one of them...'

'Or a confession by another,' Sloan finished for him.

'Kate Booth works at Fixby and Fixby, the accountants, in the high street,' announced Crosby when the inspector sent for him. 'They're on the left just beyond the Bellingham Hotel.'

'Walking distance, then,' decreed Sloan.

'There's nowhere to park down there, anyway,' said the constable grudgingly. He didn't like walking. 'And the third man in the cave that day, Simon Thornycroft, the civil engineer bloke, is working where they're building that new bridge over Calleford way although he lives in Berebury.'

'We'll get the walking over first,' decreed Sloan, ignoring the sour grapes.

Kate Booth was a plump young woman, suitably dressed in a dark professional suit, dark stockings and black shoes. She seemed to be quite pleased to be diverted from her work. 'It's not every day that you get the police calling at an accountant's office, Inspector, I can tell you.'

'I should hope not,' said Crosby righteously.

'It's usually pretty dull round here,' she said, waving her hand at a full in-tray and a bookcase filled with leather-bound tomes. 'That's why I took up caving. It's got a bit of an edge to it which accountancy hasn't.' She paused and then added, 'Unless the client hasn't been rendering unto Caesar that which is Caesar's, of course. That can get quite hairy.'

'What we'd like to know in the first instance, miss,' began Sloan without preamble, 'is whether you were at the late Derek Tridgell's funeral at Friar's Flensant?'

The thought had crossed his mind that the question was like the beginning of an algorithm: if the woman hadn't been in the church to be fixed by Paul's beady eye when he mentioned the word 'killing', then Sloan thought they could well go away again. Perhaps they could go away anyway – he wasn't sure. Although Derek Tridgell had spoken as if it had been a man who had done the killing, Sloan had been trained to remember that in matters legal the male embraced the female.

'Of course I was, Inspector,' she responded vigorously. 'All the cavers from the club were there. We sat together near the front of the church. After all, Derek had been one of us for yonks, well before I ever took up caving, anyway. I had quite a chat with his son at the wake afterwards – that's quite a good pub out at Friar's Flensant, by the way.'

'So I believe,' murmured Sloan. Any hostelry he knew would compare favourably with the canteen at the police station for a wake.

'Paul Tridgell's thinking of taking up caving now,' she chattered on, 'and following in his father's footsteps and all that. I promised I'd give him a hand when he got round to it.'

'Show him the ropes,' put in Crosby.

'Well, how to rappel down into a cave, anyway,' she said, taking this literally.

'Ah, yes,' murmured Sloan casually, 'I remember reading that you were one of those down there with Derek Tridgell when a man was killed in the Hoath Hole at Chislet Crags.'

'And not likely to forget it either, even though it was so long ago,' the young woman came back smartly. She shuddered. 'It was pretty awful at the time, I can tell you, Inspector. I couldn't stop shaking for ages.'

'Tell me,' invited Sloan, his notebook remaining just an indeterminate bulge in his pocket.

She pushed aside some papers on her desk and concentrated on her reply. 'It was something we'd been planning to do for ages – find out if there was a cave beyond the Baggles Bite. Bit of a feather in our caps at the club if we could, you know. Then we could write it up for the caving journals, too. It would have been a real speleological break-through.'

This particular behaviour Sloan could well understand. There were detectives in the Calleshire County Constabulary who went home every night and made notes for the memoirs that they would publish on their retirement. One thing he knew was that he wasn't going to be one of them. When he retired it would be a proper retirement and would be devoted to tending his roses. And perhaps one day winning a prize with them at the Berebury Flower Show.

Kate Booth said reflectively, 'We thought that there must have been something beyond that

121

squeeze even if it was just another cave, you understand. We just didn't know exactly what and we wanted to find out.'

'I see,' said Sloan, who wasn't sure that he did.

'We knew that there had to be a space of sorts,' she went on, 'because the water going through the Bite had to go somewhere.'

'It always does,' said Crosby, sitting back.

Sloan knew that water always found its own level, too, but did not feel it necessary to say so.

'There was this little streamway running through the Bite, you see, but we couldn't hear anything beyond.' She looked at both policemen. 'You understand that if there was a decent fall of water at the other side of the Bite there would be the sound of splashing?'

Detective Inspector Sloan nodded. Crosby looked bored.

She carried on. 'Of course the Bite might have gone on so long that we wouldn't have been able to hear anything anyway – we didn't even know that much about it. We couldn't see very far with a torch either because there was a bit of a dog-leg quite soon.' The telephone on her desk began to ring but she didn't answer it, her mind clearly back in the past. 'And there could either have been a lake beyond,' she opened her fingers in a gesture, 'or, as it says in *Kubla Khan*, there could have been "caverns measureless to man" running "down to a sunless sea".'

'So...?' said Sloan.

'So we decided we'd have a crack at it that Saturday.'

'Who decided?'

'I can't remember – Simon Thornycroft, I think it was, or it might have been Edmund Leaton. They were both really keen to find out what was there – we all were, actually. Had been for ages.' She looked at Sloan and grinned for the first time. 'I can't really remember who it was who suggested that we should tackle it when we did – it was one of those decisions you take together in the nearest pub at the end of a day's caving. You know how it happens.'

Detective Inspector Sloan didn't. Important decisions at the police station either took themselves in real emergencies or were debated for days before any action was taken and for days afterwards sometimes. Unfortunately the correctness of the decisions taken in either manner were accountable and stood to be argued over for months by legislators anxious to appear even-handed in the eternal battle between the actions of lesser mortals and those of the forces of law and order.

The telephone had stopped ringing.

'Go on,' he said.

'We chose the day – it was a Saturday, of course, because we were all working otherwise. And then we agreed the order we would tackle it in. There were four of us. Edmund was the slimmest and so he was to go first, then Simon, who was really the most experienced but a bit tubbier, then poor Derek...' she sighed 'and in the event it was poor Edmund, too, that day. I was just a beginner at that time and so I brought up the rear.'

'Tail-end Charlie,' put in Crosby, much attached to war films.

'Not exactly. I had been due to go third but the men changed the order at the last minute.' Kate Booth's gaze drifted towards the window and the sky. 'We had to choose a fine day in case there was flooding, which is the most dangerous thing about caving. Rain up top is always something to worry about. There was a good forecast for that Saturday, though, which is why we settled on it.'

'Of course,' murmured Sloan. 'Go on.'

'We'd had to rappel down – the cave was quite deep at that point – when we went in it for the first time but we'd fixed some ladders for the proper attempt after that to make access easier. We had to watch out when we got to the cave floor because there were lots of speleothems about.'

'Come again?' interrupted Crosby.

Kate Booth explained. 'Stalactites and stalagmites.'

'The tights come down and the mites climb up,' chanted Crosby joyously.

'What we had to do,' said the young accountant seriously, 'was keep well clear of them. Not done, you know, to break 'em off. We had to be careful anyway because there were a lot of big stones and rubble on the cave floor too. There must have been an earlier roof fall there at some time or other. No idea when, naturally.'

The telephone started ringing again but she still didn't answer it, her mind a long way away in the past.

'Edmund got into the Bite all right and was making good progress, although you could see that the way was getting a bit tight at this point because of the dog-leg beginning. We saw his light disappearing round it and then...' She stopped abruptly, an unhappy grimace overtaking her face as memory flooded back.

'And then?' prompted Sloan gently.

'And then,' she said, 'Simon's headlight went out and it went a bit dark.'

'Like that canary in the coal mine,' said Crosby, 'that snuffed it when things went wrong.'

Kate Booth ignored this. 'Simon fiddled about with it for a bit and then he called back over his shoulder to Derek and me to tell us to stop where we were while he crawled back to Derek to get a light from his torch so he could put a new battery in. He'd just got back to us when there was this great big bang and the roof of the Bite came down, crushing Edmund.' Her eyes dimmed with tears. 'Derek pushed past Simon because he'd got a light and Simon hadn't, of course, and started to scrabble at the roof fall but it was hopeless. Quite hopeless.'

Detective Inspector Sloan, having read the newspaper report of the inquest, nodded that he understood.

'There was just a solid wall of fallen rock in front of us,' she said tearfully. 'Simon followed in Derek's light and tried to help clear a way, too, but it was no good. No good at all.'

'And dangerous,' said Sloan.

'I don't think any of us thought about that at first,' she said frankly, 'but what did get dangerous quite soon after the roof fall happened was the Bite getting blocked. The stream started to build up pretty quickly in front of the roof fall and we knew we would all drown if we didn't get out pronto.' Her face crumpled. 'So we had to leave poor Edmund buried there and back out to higher ground fast.'

'Or you'd have been goners, too,' observed Crosby matter-of-factly.

She started to cry. 'The last I saw of Edmund,' she gulped, 'was the soles of his boots going into the Bite and I haven't been able to get the memory of them out of my mind ever since.' She shivered. 'There was a funny smell about, too, like marzipan and whenever I smell that now it brings it all back. Silly, isn't it?'

CHAPTER TWELVE

There was no doubt about it, Detective Constable Crosby fancied himself in a hard white hat. Happily, wearing one had been the first requirement of stepping on-site at the bridgeworks at North Caughton Marsh. That was long before they found anyone who was prepared to direct the two policemen to where Simon Thornycroft might be found.

The constable wore his hard hat tilted at an angle that could only be described as jaunty and clearly saw it as an improvement on any other head gear that he had ever worn. Simon Thornycroft was wearing one, too, but his was set squarely on his head, while both his arms were extended as he clasped a partially unrolled plan between his hands. The plan was proving unruly in the wind

126

and hard to hold. He was standing in white over-alls considering a half-built caisson on the north bank of the River Calle when the two policemen reached him.

A girl in a mobile office had directed them to the civil engineer. 'He's pretty busy,' she had said dubiously. 'He doesn't like being disturbed while he's working. And,' she added, 'if you hear a maroon go off, watch out for blasting.'

Simon Thornycroft, though, was amiable enough when they got to him, starting to roll up the plan as they approached. 'Police? What can I do for you, gentlemen?'

Detective Inspector Sloan, his own hard hat perched uncomfortably over a full head of hair, launched smoothly into a spiel about checking up on some old cases, including that of the death of Edmund Leaton.

'Edmund Leaton?' echoed Thornycroft, clearly puzzled. He rolled the map up. 'That was a long time ago, Inspector.'

'Five or six years or more, sir,' agreed Sloan easily. 'As you will know, the inquest was adjourned *sine die.*'

Thornycroft looked quite startled. 'His body hasn't been found surely? Not under all that limestone. Or has there been another rockfall?'

'No, sir. The matter came up again because it was mentioned at Derek Tridgell's funeral.'

'Ah, yes, of course.' He nodded and said 'Indeed, I talked about it myself. Well, I can tell you that Derek did a damn good job that day.' He sighed. 'Not that it did any good.'

'Tell me,' said Sloan.

Thornycroft, having rolled up the plan, tucked it under his arm, naval fashion, and said, 'Getting through that squeeze – the Baggles Bite, it's called in the club – would have been a real speleological prize for us and we'd all been itching to have a go at it for a long while.'

Detective Inspector Sloan could readily understand the attraction of this and said so: there were famous unsolved criminal cases whose solutions were dangling somewhere just out of police reach. Feathers waiting to be pinned to caps was how he thought of them. And he didn't only mean the famous William Herbert Wallace case.

'And one evening in the pub,' went on Thornycroft, 'when we were sitting around chatting, we decided to have a try at it the following weekend. We'd put some ladders in for when we made our proper attempt.'

'We?'

'Edmund, Derek, a young girl called Kate Booth – it was her first big venture – and myself. Edmund was leading because he was on the skinny side and a dab hand at getting through tight spots, me following, and then Derek, with Kate bringing up the rear.'

'Ladies last,' observed Crosby, once brought to task by female Police Sergeant Perkins for holding a door open for her. She was perfectly capable, she had barked, of opening the door for herself.

'Kate was a bit of a rock chick even in those days, but still quite inexperienced, though she's got pretty good since,' went on Thornycroft. 'Anyway we got down to the cave floor and then went down quite a lot further, short step.'

'Short step?'

'Oh, sorry, Inspector. It's an army term for marching downhill.'

Sloan, Head of the Criminal Investigation Department, nodded. The uniformed branch of the police, white gloves and all, marched when civic occasion demanded it. Detectives didn't.

'There was quite a slope downwards to begin with, Inspector, and there was a great deal of breakdown there to cover before we got to the Bite...'

'Breakdown?'

'Lots of odd rocks – some pretty big ones and some small – that had fallen down from the roof onto the cave floor. The trouble is that that particular breakdown could have been fifty thousand years ago or last week and if you're a caver you don't always know which.'

'You mean it could happen again?' asked Crosby, wide-eyed.

'Any time,' said Thornycroft soberly. 'And it did, of course, further on in the cave and a bit later that day. It's one of the dangers of caving. Not the only one, of course.'

'Was the roof known to be in a dangerous condition, sir?'

'Not that we knew about at the time,' said Thornycroft frankly. 'We'd never got beyond the dog-leg before which is what made it such an interesting proposition. And,' he added, 'if we'd known the roof was unstable we'd never have gone in there in the first place.'

'And then?' prompted Sloan.

'Edmund went into the squeeze first and he

129

was making good progress – the last we saw of him were the soles of his boots as he inched his way forwards into the Bite and round the dog-leg. Then the light in my headlamp went out just before I was going to follow him in. I called back to Derek Tridgell to tell him to stop where he was while I went back to get Derek to help me load a new battery. It's very difficult to do it without any light at all down there, you understand.'

'I can imagine it would be,' said Detective Inspector Sloan, who realised he actually knew nothing about the depths of Stygian gloom to be found in a deep cave without any light.

'And I couldn't risk dropping the new battery in the water, you see. Oh, did I tell you there was a little stream running through the squeeze? We'd already tried putting a whole lot of fluorescein in it...'

'Fluorescein?' asked Sloan, who had a deep-rooted objection to the use of words that he wasn't likely to know by other people.

'Sorry, Inspector. It's a dye. We really wanted to see first exactly where the stream came out of the caves and made its way to the river Calle and the sea – if it ever surfaced anywhere at all, that is.'

Something stirred in Detective Inspector Sloan's memory at the combined mention of rocks, dye and the sea. It was a line heard in his schooldays and one that had made the class of boys laugh – he remembered that much. He searched his mind now, only giving Simon Thornycroft's account half an ear.

Smooth Adonis – that was the image that had had the class so tickled. And it came from John

130

Milton's *Paradise Lost* which had amused them even more. The schoolmaster had explained that in legend Adonis was a beautiful boy and would have been naked – smooth – and therefore purple with cold when he ran into the sea, hence the line 'Smooth Adonis from his native rock/Ran purple to the sea'. Perhaps, thought Sloan, the fluorescein had run purple to the sea, too.

Either way, he was prepared to bet that it was the only line any of the class – including him – still remembered. An older, sadder, wiser and more experienced Christopher Dennis Sloan, police officer, was ready to worry now more about the way in which the schoolmaster had dwelt overlong on the image of a beautiful naked boy running into the sea. Where Milton came in, he didn't know.

'But,' Simon Thornycroft was continuing, 'the dye doesn't always surface and, in this case, it didn't.'

'What goes down must come up,' pronounced Crosby, rather pleased with himself.

'Not if the stream is in a phreatic tube,' responded Thornycroft, hastily going on to explain that that meant that it could be running along below the water table and not come out anywhere where it could be seen, what was called 'secret water'. 'The limestone over there's riddled with caves – it's a hard rock but permeable, you see. There's fourteen miles of them down there under the crags – and no end of streams.'

Sloan hauled the man back to his narrative. 'Edmund Leaton...'

'Edmund just disappeared mostly out of sight round the dog-leg in the squeeze, Inspector, like

131

I told you, when there was a sudden whoosh and the roof of the Bite – heaven alone knows how much of it – collapsed on him. We couldn't see Edmund at all then, not even his boots. Derek crawled straight past me – he had a light, you see – and started to pull away at the rock with his bare hands but it was hopeless.' He shook his head. 'Quite hopeless. I came up behind him but I couldn't do anything either. And then...' he broke off and fell silent.

'And then,' prompted Sloan.

'And then, Inspector, we suddenly started to get very wet. Kate shouted to us that we needed to get out fast. The rockfall had blocked the stream, you see, and the water was backing up in front of it quite quickly as that part of the cave flooded. We turned round and scrambled back towards the higher ground as quickly as we could.' Thornycroft shook himself as if to rid his mind of the memory. 'It was quite worrying but eventually we got back up the ladders to the ledge above and then out to daylight but it took time. There was nothing left to do except call the police, and,' he added bleakly, 'go and tell poor Amelia.'

'Amelia?'

'His wife.' He winced. 'God, I can tell you, Inspector, that was quite awful ... I've never forgotten it.'

'Sorry to drag you all round here after work,' said Paul Tridgell to the other two men who had convened in the living room of Elizabeth Shelford's bungalow. 'Not all actually,' he explained, 'because I haven't asked Danny Saville to join us.

That's because he doesn't really know us.'

'Luckily for him,' muttered Tim Cullen, one of the four there. 'I bet he wishes he'd never set eyes on any of us.'

'I'm sure he does. After all, it was really dark when he got in the car that night and he's been quite out of it since the accident,' agreed Paul.

'He isn't the only one,' said Trevor Skewis sourly. 'I swear my head's not right yet.'

Elizabeth said, 'Count yourself very lucky that it's still on your shoulders, Trevor. It nearly mightn't have been.'

'Sorry, Liz,' he apologised to her. 'I should have thought before I opened my big mouth.'

Elizabeth, old before her time now, thought that applied to almost everyone who had spoken to her after the accident but she held her peace. That was something else she had learnt to do the hard way.

'That's what we all need to do,' insisted Paul urgently. He turned to Trevor Skewis. 'Not open our big mouths, I mean. It's all a matter of keeping our heads and thinking before we speak. One word out of turn and one of us here could go to prison for up to fourteen years. You do realise that, don't you all?'

A little silence descended on the quartet. Presently Paul broke it by asking if anyone had had the police round lately.

Trevor Skewis and Tim Cullen both shook their heads.

'Well, you will,' forecast Paul. 'And very soon, probably. They've already been to see me and Elizabeth.'

She nodded. 'Two of them came here, wanting to know about the accident all over again. They said they were detectives.'

'Why?' asked Trevor. 'I mean, why now? And why detectives?'

'I thought that it was all over bar the shouting,' Tim Cullen caught sight of a bleak look in Elizabeth's eye and hastily amended this to, 'I meant to say when all was done and dusted.' He realised that this was hardly more tactful and blushed to the roots of his hair.

'After all,' said Trevor, 'it looked to me as if they'd gone through everything possible at the time. They were pretty thorough then.'

Tim gave a visible shudder. 'You can say that again, mate. I couldn't believe how horrible the coroner was at Bill's inquest. Talk about the Spanish Inquisition – I still wake up in the night thinking about it.'

Another silence fell on the quartet. The emotional effects of the accident were by common consent a taboo subject and never mentioned. Post-traumatic stress syndrome had been strenuously denied by them all.

'Something's stirred the police up all over again,' said Paul. He had come out of the tragic evening the least physically damaged of all of them. No one was going to be allowed to suspect how affected in other ways he had been. 'The trouble is we don't know what it is that's got them going second time round.' Paul did know, but he wasn't going to tell the others.

Tim looked out of the window at the gathering darkness and got to his feet. 'I'd like to get going now, if it's all the same with you people. I'm on duty tonight.' He turned at the door, his hand on the handle and admitted self-consciously, 'Actually I haven't got back to driving yet. No car, these days. But there's a bus due any minute now.'

Trevor pulled the corners of his mouth down and mumbled that he'd got back to driving but he didn't enjoy it any more. 'It's not like it used to be. The fun's gone out of it these days. I'll hang on a bit longer though, Elizabeth, if it's all right with you.'

'I haven't driven since because I've lost that first fine careless rapture, too, even though I've got that adapted car,' said the girl astringently. 'But you can stay.'

'I don't want to be late either,' said Paul tactfully. 'I've promised to take my sister down to the Lamb and Flag for a drink tonight.' He added seriously, 'On foot.'

CHAPTER THIRTEEN

'Well, Sloan, are we dealing with a popcorn thriller or aren't we?' demanded Superintendent Leeyes the next morning from the comfort of his own office. The barrier of a sizeable desk between him and his subordinate served still further to fortify the impression of his overriding authority. It was a very different scenario from standing, windswept, in a marsh beside a river, thought Sloan, trying to interview a patently busy man

135

about something that had happened in a cave a long time before.

'A popcorn thriller, sir?' said Sloan. 'I'm afraid that...'

'One where you're too frightened to chew popcorn while you're watching the film,' expanded the superintendent. 'Ghastly stuff, of course. Popcorn, I mean, not that I suppose the film is ever any better. I never touch it myself.'

'No, sir. Naturally. Of course not.' Sloan hesitated. 'I'm not quite sure that I take your meaning though...'

'A really exciting thriller, Sloan,' Leeyes declared, 'keeps your mind on the screen not on your belly. So, have we got a real thriller on our hands or is this whole business a figment of the imagination of a dying man?'

'I'm not sure yet, sir. All I can say at this stage is that I'm certain the son doesn't think so, although he strenuously denies staring at anyone in particular when he read out that bit about it being a time to kill.'

'In any case,' said Leeyes tetchily, 'I'm afraid that his stressing of the word "kill" at the funeral and glaring at someone unknown hardly amounts to evidence likely to convince the Crown Prosecution Service that they have a winnable case.'

'I agree that it's not a lot to go on, sir,' conceded the detective inspector.

'A bite-sized clue if ever there was one,' grumbled Leeyes. 'And there's that Ponzi scheme over at Pelling that needs looking into before any more fools and their money are parted.'

'Yes, sir.' Sloan was the first to agree that it had

been a very small clue at Friar's Flensant if ever there was one and said so.

'And did you get anywhere with the wrong remainderman that the deceased had talked about?'

'No, sir.' Actually Sloan thought the expression 'Last man standing' described a remainderman best. He didn't see how anyone could get that wrong. You were the last or you weren't.

'And you say the man's widow and daughter still insist that they have no idea what the deceased was talking about?'

'None. It was they who sent for us.'

'That figures, otherwise,' concluded Superintendent Leeyes, worldly-wise, 'they wouldn't have needed to have told us a dicky-bird about it.' The superintendent drummed his fingers on his desk. 'And now that you say that you've followed up all your leads, what do you think?'

'The deceased was only actually present at one of the deaths – the one down the Chislet Caves...' began Sloan, notebook at the ready.

'Caves, did you say?' Leeyes sat up. 'Plato had a lot to say about caves.'

'Really, sir?' said Sloan. That must have come from a course on history, myths and legends attended briefly – very briefly – by the superintendent one winter. The brevity of his attendance had been spectacular even by the superintendent's track record (and there had been a happy winner of a sweepstake at the police station who had gone for the lowest numbers).

If Sloan remembered correctly it had foundered on the moment when Leeyes had had Oedipus's history spelt out by the lecturer. The superintendent, whose views on sentencing were widely known in 'F' Division and by the magistrates on the Berebury bench, had declared that Oedipus's killing of his father, marrying his mother and siring four of her children had merited greater punishment than easy exile.

'Plato had these prisoners chained in a cave so that they could only look at a wall,' Leeyes informed him now.

'Indeed, sir?' Sloan tried to sound interested. Police contact with prisons was deliberately kept at an absolute minimum.

'So that all that the prisoners were able to see were the shadows of people walking in front of a fire that was behind them.'

'Very confusing, I'm sure, sir.'

'Stopped them dealing with reality,' said Leeyes, summing up in a very few words a famous allegory of Plato as narrated by Socrates.

'The shadow not the substance?' offered Detective Inspector Sloan tentatively.

'Exactly, Sloan. And that's what I think you're dealing with.'

'Yes, sir.' He hurried on, his further investigation of the Ponzi scheme at Pelling looming ever nearer, 'As I was saying, sir, Derek Tridgell was in a cave under Chislet Crags when a man was killed and might have been present at a chemical firm when another man died – we can't confirm that yet – but there was also someone at the wheel of a car who killed a man and Derek Tridgell's son was one of those in that car.'

'Don't haver, man.'

138

'I have also, sir, been trying to work out the significance of Derek Tridgell using the word "killed" and not "murdered".'

'If any,' said Leeyes flatly.

'Killing would include the driver of the car, sir. Someone died – was killed – in that accident and Derek Tridgell might have known who was at the wheel.'

'Or been told.'

'Or even guessed,' sighed Sloan. 'After all, sir, that son of his took himself off to South America very soon after the accident.'

'What about his mother?' asked Leeyes. 'Does she know?'

'If she does, sir, she isn't saying,' said Sloan, adding, 'but I think that some of the survivors of that accident know all right. That's half the trouble, and they aren't saying anything either.'

Sloan closed the door of Superintendent Leeyes' room behind him with care. The thought of getting back to the peace and quiet of his own office came as a real relief after trying to follow his superior officer's tortuous way of thinking. Half of his own mind was still meditating on the words of a dying man at Friar's Flensant but – conscientious working detective that he was – the other half was already beginning to turn towards the possible financial fraud out at Pelling. There was at least nothing urgent about what Derek Tridgell had said but even now gullible people might be being deprived of their life's savings, which was undoubtedly urgent.

Detective Constable Crosby was there in his

office waiting for him. 'It's Inspector Harpe, sir. He said would you please ring him as soon as.'

Sloan picked up the internal telephone on the instant. 'That you, Harry? What's up?'

'Ah, Seedy, glad to have got you. Listen, you were interested in a man called Paul Tridgell, weren't you?'

'What about him?' said Sloan immediately. 'What about him?'

'He was in that pile-up last Christmas, remember? The one we spoke about. Well, I have news for you.'

Sloan pulled his notebook in front of him on the desk, pen poised. 'Tell me.'

'He and his sister were walking home from their local out at Friar's Flensant last night.'

'The Lamb and Flag Inn,' supplied Sloan.

'That's the place. There's a stretch of road there without a pavement and, of course, being out in the sticks like it is in the village, there isn't any street lighting either.'

'Go on.' Sloan's pen hovered over his notebook.

'It seems a car came up from behind them and knocked Paul Tridgell over. He was walking on the outside, of course.'

There wasn't any 'of course' about it these days but this was neither the time nor the place to be talking about the courteous behaviour of Englishmen of yesteryear in walking on the outside to shelter their ladies from passing traffic.

'The car didn't touch the sister although it seems she fell forward, too,' Harpe was going on, 'but Tridgell's badly bruised all over and they're not sure whether he's broken his wrist or not.

He'll be out of action for a bit anyway.'

'Which is presumably what someone wanted,' said Sloan, thinking aloud. 'That's if it wasn't an accident.'

'Could be,' said Harry Harpe. 'Your department, that, Seedy. Not mine. The hospital says he'll be all right when the bruises go down – they're going to take another look at his X-rays this morning – but, having examined the scene myself last night, I'd say that it was a pretty close-run thing. It looks as if the driver didn't slow down at all – there's not a skid mark in sight.'

'Make of car?'

'You're joking. That sister of his...'

'Jane.'

'I understand she's an art student which should have made her observant but take it from me, her eye does not extend to the make of motor vehicles. All she can remember is that she thought the car was black...'

A saying about all cats being black in the dark flitted through Sloan's mind but he didn't voice it.

'And that it didn't stop,' finished the traffic inspector. 'She knew that, all right.'

'Ah.' Both policemen knew that that was what mattered.

'The casualty himself was a bit more spot on,' admitted Harpe grudgingly. 'He said he looked for the number plate as he fell and realised that it was being driven without lights. No tail lights to be seen.'

'So it was no accident,' concluded Sloan.

'Nope, because he was also aware of something

141

else. It didn't dawn on him though until the hospital had finished with him.'

'What was that?' The page in Sloan's notebook was filling up.

'He thought that the dashboard lights might have been covered over – there was no light showing in the vehicle at all. Hence no light reflected on the driver's face.'

'He'd only need to be masked to be totally unidentifiable, then,' said Sloan.

'He certainly might have been but don't forget, Seedy, there's still the car.' In the admittedly jaundiced view of the traffic inspector, evidence gleaned from vehicles was more reliable than that from human beings. For one thing, machines didn't change the story that they'd told.

'Glass on the road?' asked Sloan, perking up. What could be learnt by forensic specialists from broken glass was a constant source of wonder to him.

'None, which was interesting in itself. You can tape a headlight all over, you know, so that it doesn't shatter on impact.'

'Tyre marks?'

'Not many since, as I said, the driver doesn't seem to have braked at all and what marks that are there are a darn side too common to be much help but, rest assured, Seedy, we've put the word out this morning. Anyone taking a car with a damaged nearside front wing into a garage anywhere any time soon is going to be reported to us pretty pronto.'

Detective Inspector Sloan thanked his friend, folded his notebook shut and put away his pen. It had, he noted, taken less than five minutes to put a potential fraud at Pelling completely out of his mind.

CHAPTER FOURTEEN

At much the same time Jonathon Sharp was welcoming Chris Honley into his office at Berebury Pharmaceuticals. The chairman belonged to the tidy desk school of business management – there was just the one sheet of paper in front of him and so far there was nothing whatsoever written on it.

'Come along in and sit down, Honley,' he said, waving an inviting arm in the direction of a standard office chair the other side of his desk. There were no easy chairs placed cosily side by side in front of a low coffee table for informal chats in Jonathon Sharp's room. The decor was totally businesslike. And there was no doubt either about who was in charge. 'I've told Marion Tridgell about your coming here from Luston Chemicals and that we wanted you to get stuck in as soon as possible.' He gave him an encouraging smile. 'There's nothing stopping you settling down here now your gardening leave's up.'

'How did she take it?' asked Honley curiously. 'After all, it's all been a bit quick, her husband having only just died.'

'She was very calm about your coming, as I thought she would be. She said she didn't know you but had heard about your good work at Luston Chemicals. She quite understood that you wouldn't want to stay on there after what had happened to poor Michael Linane.'

Ralph Iddon, the Luston firm's chairman, hadn't been anything like as calm about Chris Honley's jumping ship from his own outfit – especially to his going to that particular firm too – but the chemist saw no reason to tell his new employer this.

Honley shuddered now. 'No way was I going to stay there. Not ever.'

'Their loss, our gain,' beamed Sharp benevolently.

'At least you say Marion Tridgell understands how I felt which is more than Ralph Iddon seemed to,' said Honley bitterly. 'He's got no fine feelings, that man.'

'She's a sensible woman,' said Sharp, tapping his desk with his pen, 'which is more than you could say for Paul, that son of hers. He's much too uptight for his own good.' That he thought Paul Tridgell might be a bit of a problem to anybody else as well he did not mention to the man sitting in front of him.

'He must be quite young still,' said the other man tolerantly.

'I think in a way,' went on Jonathon Sharp, following his own train of thought, 'Marion's lost interest in the firm now, apart from Derek's pension, of course. Drawn the shutters down on the past and all that but still, of course, very proud of what he did for Ameliorite.'

'Quite right, too,' said Honley warmly. 'It was a

144

really elegant product from a pharmaceutical point of view. Derek Tridgell knew his job, all right, and he did you proud over here. By the way, what's going to happen to Ameliorite now?'

Sharp sighed. 'Token production only – you can't fight predatory pricing, you know. By the time you've won your court case you'll already have gone to the wall. Since your sainted lot at Luston undercut us, the product's dead in the water, blast them.'

'Well, I hope to do as well for Berebury Pharmaceuticals as poor Derek did – by the way, what are we going to call what I'll be working on?'

Jonathon Sharp drummed his fingers on his desk. 'Good question.'

'Or do you just want it still only to have a number?'

The chairman shook his head. 'I don't like numbers – people get them wrong too easily. The fat finger syndrome and all that. No, a name would be better.'

'It's got to have a name that won't mean anything to anyone poking about,' insisted Honley. 'Not like Ameliorite, which does what it says on the tin – ameliorates pain. Or Mendaner, come to that. The trouble with all doctors,' he added bitterly, 'is that they only see pain as a symptom, not as a problem to the patient.'

Sharp stared at his desk for a long minute and then took up his pen, a little smile twitching his lips. 'I know – we'll call it after something to do with caving as a sort of tribute to Derek. That should put anyone off the scent.'

'Good idea,' said Honley, sitting back comfortably in his chair. 'I'd heard that going down holes in the ground was his thing.'

'He took me down the caves at Chislet Crags once and that was quite enough,' shuddered Sharp. 'I could never see the attraction myself but he used to say that you needed a touch of danger in your life to keep you on your toes. Like that philosopher who thought it was good for you to live on the side of a volcano.'

'Rather him than me. I was told that he was a great caver, though.'

'He thought caving was the perfect antidote to pharmaceutical research,' said Sharp. 'I can't understand why myself. A dirty and dangerous hobby, if you ask me.'

'Life in the lab can be a touch unexciting from time to time,' said Chris Honley moderately.

'I hope it isn't going to be with you here,' responded his new boss immediately. 'We've got a lot riding on you, Honley, and I'd like your time here to be very exciting and our new project successful.'

'So what are we going to call it, then?' asked Chris Honley again. 'It needs a name or people won't think I'm actually doing any work.'

'You'll be doing that, all right, Honley, and getting cracking very soon, I hope.'

'A name, then.'

'One of Derek's favourite caving words was "Resurgence".'

'Resurgence,' Chris Honley rolled the word round his tongue. 'A coming back – yes, that would do nicely.'

'He explained once that it meant going down

one hole, through a range of caves and then coming out of another hole, usually wet through.'

'Sounds great,' said Honley sardonically.

A very different aspect of business behaviour was emerging in the industrial town of Luston. It was being projected by Ralph Iddon, Chairman of Luston Chemicals, and this became very evident when David Heath, newly appointed replacement of the late lamented Michael Linane as his head of sales, reported to him. Iddon's office could not have been in greater contrast to that of Jonathon Sharp. The word that described it best was plush. The carpet was thick and the walls hung with modern art. Although his desk was polished walnut, Iddon was not sitting at it. Instead he was settled in a padded chair at the other side of the room, under a watercolour painting of the River Calle, nursing a cup of coffee and notably relaxed.

'Sales of Mendaner are going up,' said the head of sales, shuffling a sheaf of papers in his hands. He offered a sheet of figures across the coffee table but Ralph Iddon waved it away. 'But the profit on it is way down,' said Heath.

Ralph Iddon rubbed his hands together.

'Big time,' stressed his salesman. 'Both of them are up – sales and losses.'

'The more the merrier of both, David,' said Iddon. 'Think what they must be losing over at Berebury Pharmaceuticals.'

The new head of sales said that nevertheless the situation was playing merry hell with his own figures and he didn't like it.

Ralph Iddon ignored him. 'Berebury Pharmaceuticals can't be selling any of their Ameliorite at all these days.'

'Not at their price, anyway,' agreed David Heath.

'Not at our price, which is what matters,' said the chairman happily. 'I can see that your trouble, David, is that you don't have any appetite for risk.'

'Probably not,' said his head of sales, mindful of his bonus. Risk wasn't meant to go with sales – its requirements were enthusiasm, contacts, good publicity, a reliable supply chain, cast-iron back-up and, above all, a first-class product. He decided against saying any of this to his boss.

'You have to look at the big picture, David,' said Ralph Iddon, whose mind was following quite a different train of thought.

'Sure,' responded David, notably unenthusiastic.

'And,' went on Iddon, rubbing his hands to-gether again, 'the Berebury lot certainly can't afford to match our prices, let alone undercut us. No way. As I said before, remember, you have to look at the big picture.'

'So you say,' said his head of sales even more tepidly.

'Moreover,' chortled Iddon, 'they must have been left with all their stock of their unsold pro-duct on their hands into the bargain.'

David Heath nodded and said neutrally, 'I agree that Ameliorite must have gone to the wall by now.'

Ralph Iddon shied away from that particular metaphor like a nervous horse and said quickly, 'I think we've practically cornered the market by now.'

'At quite a cost, though,' the salesman reminded him. He would have also liked to remind the chairman that cornering a market was illegal, something vague about the history of Zanzibar and cloves coming to his own mind. As it was, he thought that Luston Chemicals might be sailing pretty close to the wind but he didn't feel he had been at the firm long enough to voice an opinion. Especially that one. And, as his wife was always reminding him, there was his bonus to bear in mind. That was worth more than a consciously suppressed view.

'Don't you worry about the cost,' Iddon was going on bracingly. 'Oh, I know it's your job to keep an eye on costs and sales, David, and I know you do it very well but remember that as soon as Jonathon Sharp stops producing his stuff altogether we move in, put our price well up and make a real killing. That's the name of the game.'

What he didn't say aloud was that with any luck the loss of their star product, Ameliorite, would also bring about the total collapse of their great rival, Berebury Pharmaceuticals.

CHAPTER FIFTEEN

Detective Inspector Sloan thanked his friend, Harry Harpe, and made his way back to his own office, thinking hard the while. Detective Constable Crosby was still there doing, as far as Sloan could see, nothing at all.

'Into action, Crosby,' said Sloan crisply.

The constable sprang to his feet, clearly equating action with travel. 'Where to, sir?'

'Legate Lodge, Friar's Flensant,' said Sloan, 'to see a young man about an apparent attack on his person.'

'Not that Paul Tridgell?' asked Crosby hopefully.

'None other,' said Sloan, reminding himself of the importance of a police officer remaining detached and impartial throughout an investigation. He toyed with the idea of emphasising this to Crosby but that callow young officer was already halfway out of the door making for the police car and thus was well out of earshot.

'He needed taking down a peg or two,' said Crosby, strapping himself in to the car. 'Too cocky by half, if you ask me.'

'I must remind you, Crosby,' said Sloan sternly, 'that the law requires that a police officer should be *"idoneous homo"* as well as, I trust, *"sapiens"*.'

'Come again, sir.' Crosby steered the car out into the traffic swirling round the exit to the police station, pleased as ever to see that it gave way to the police car as it usually did. He enjoyed the deference.

'Have the honesty to execute the office of constable without malice, affection or partiality,' said Sloan, quoting his old station sergeant's legal hero, Patrick Colquhoun.

'I still think he's too cocky by half,' said Crosby rebelliously. Clear of the town, he put his foot down and shot off in the direction of Friar's Flensant.

150

'He may have his reasons,' said Sloan absently. He had already added that young man's behaviour to the growing list of imponderables in his mind.

Marion Tridgell admitted them to the house, looking worried. 'What on earth is going on, Inspector? Jane and Paul could both have been killed last night. They really will have to do something about that road now.'

Detective Inspector Sloan nodded and agreed that the road could do with street lighting and a pavement. He decided against explaining at this point that this was a matter for the county highway authority, whose interest in rural roads was known to be minimal. And that the state of the roadway was probably not relevant in this instance.

'But surely,' she went on, 'any driver should have seen two pedestrians in his headlights even though it was in the dark.'

Sloan believed in truth over tact. 'I understand from what your son told our traffic people last night that the car was being driven without lights.' The impious thought that Paul Tridgell had thus made it abundantly clear to Inspector Harpe that therefore he couldn't be expected to help identify the car or driver Sloan kept to himself for the time being.

'You mean that the driver meant to hit Paul and Jane?' she said, visibly stricken.

'Paul, anyway, perhaps,' temporised Sloan. 'May I see him?'

Paul Tridgell was lying on the sofa in the sitting room, whilst his sister was huddled into an armchair near the fireplace, somehow seeming smaller than Sloan had remembered her.

'I'm stirred, Inspector,' Paul announced grandly from the depths of the sofa, waving his left arm in Sloan's direction, 'but not shaken.' His face and hands were covered in grazes and his right wrist heavily bandaged. He was obviously, too, taking great care not to move his right knee.

In Sloan's opinion, Paul Tridgell was not only stirred but considerably shaken as well. His hands displayed a tiny tremor and his voice was high and indignant. He asked Paul if he knew of anyone who would deliberately want to knock him down.

His answer came too soon and too emphatically.

'Certainly not, Inspector. I may not be like Rudyard Kipling's *Kim* – the little friend of all the world – but I don't know of any enemies.'

'That's a pity,' said Sloan pleasantly, 'because it rather looks as if you might have one at least.'

Marion Tridgell had come into the room behind him. 'Jane was luckier, though,' she said, indicating her daughter who was curled up in an easy chair on the other side of the room in what an expert would have called the foetal position. 'Weren't you, dear?'

'If you call being pitched to the ground in the dark from behind out of the blue while Paul got hit beside me being lucky,' she said pallidly. 'I don't.'

'At least you landed on the grass verge,' said her brother, waving his grazed hands in front of her. 'I hit the road.'

'I thought Paul was dead when I first saw him lying there in the road,' said Jane tremulously. 'It was awful.'

'Don't,' pleaded Marion.

'Well, I wasn't dead, was I?' said her brother irritably. He turned to Sloan and demanded to know when the police were going to trace the driver of the car.

'All in good time, sir.'

Paul Tridgell gave a derisory snort.

'However,' Sloan carried on firmly, 'I am given to understand by my colleague in Traffic Division that in the first instance you were very much against the police being sent for at all last night.'

The young man on the sofa began, 'I didn't feel too bad at first...'

'I wanted the police and the ambulance to come,' Jane interrupted him plaintively. 'And as quickly as possible. Both of them.'

Detective Inspector Sloan swept on regardless. 'Moreover, Inspector Harpe tells me that in fact it was a passing motorist who sent for us and for an ambulance, too, in spite of your asking him not to, Mr Tridgell. Perhaps you could explain this.'

'Didn't want to make a fuss,' muttered Paul.

'But you might have been killed, both of you,' protested his mother. 'Don't you understand?'

'Well, I wasn't killed,' he said ungraciously. 'Was I?'

'Or broken your wrist,' she said, still unhappy.

'I haven't done that either.' He tried to wave his bandaged arm in the air to demonstrate this movement but was patently defeated by pain. 'The hospital said this morning that it's only a very bad sprain and that it'll be all right in a day or so. So will my knee.'

'And poor Jane could have been harmed,' his mother persisted, looking across at the somehow diminished figure in the armchair. 'This is very serious, Paul, and you shouldn't trivialise it.'

'All I want to know,' said Paul grumpily, 'is when the police are going to find the maniac who very nearly killed us last night.'

Detective Inspector Sloan changed the subject. 'Can all three of you now assure me once again that you know of no reason why your late husband and father should have said what he did about someone killing someone?'

He knew what their answers to the question would be before he asked it. What he wanted to see was the exchange of glances between the three of them as he spoke. He was rewarded by seeing a quick look pass between mother and son and an insistent shake of the head by the girl in the armchair, who didn't try to meet anyone's eye.

'No idea,' said Paul quickly.

'We would have told you before, Inspector,' said Marion with quiet dignity, 'had we known.'

The personal mobile telephone in Sloan's pocket began to ring. 'Excuse me,' he said to the Tridgells, slipping out of the room and into the hall, leaving Crosby to listen to anything the family said when he wasn't there.

It was Inspector Harpe on his phone. 'Hi, Seedy, another bit of news for you.'

'Go on.'

'A male customer turned up at the Leopard's Head garage at Almstone first thing this morning with a damaged nearside front wing.'

'Did he, indeed?' said Sloan, tugging his note-book out of his pocket.

'Black car, too.'

'Well, well.'

'He told the man at the garage that he'd hit a brick gate pillar as he turned into his entrance at home.'

'And you've got a name and address for me, haven't you?'

'You bet. He's called Trevor Skewis and he lives at Oakwood Close, Larking.'

'Which,' said Sloan, 'is not a Sabbath day's march from Friar's Flensant.'

'Too right. He lives at Number 13, as it happens.'

'Thanks a lot, Harry. The number 13 might just be lucky for us.'

'And in case you've forgotten, Seedy, Skewis was the surname of one of those guys in that fatal last Christmas that we talked about.'

'I hadn't forgotten,' said Detective Inspector Sloan before ringing off.

'Trevor Skewis, sir?' asked Crosby as the two policemen left the Tridgell household and set off back to Berebury. 'Who's he?'

'One of those in the same fatal road traffic accident as Paul Tridgell last Christmastime, remember?' said Detective Inspector Sloan.

'Aha,' said Crosby.

'That,' responded Sloan astringently, 'puts it very well. On the other hand, Crosby, it is always a mistake to theorise ahead of data and you should always remember that.'

'Beg pardon, sir?'

'Never mind,' sighed Sloan. 'But, if you remember, Crosby, he is also a man whom we were told was at our Paul's father's funeral. So was someone called Tim Cullen, don't forget. We'll have to see him next.'

'So this Skewis fellow might have been the one that got the evil eye,' concluded the detective constable, whose reading included the wilder sides of literature.

'Perhaps, but only perhaps, Crosby. Remember that, too.' He put his mobile phone back in his pocket and said, 'I'm told that Trevor Skewis is a trainee dispenser at that big chemist's shop in the high street. Inspector Harpe tells me that he heard that he had had to take a bus from Almstone to work this morning while the damaged wing of his car was repaired.'

'Tough,' said Crosby, who rarely took a bus either.

Privately Sloan thought this may not be the only thing that Trevor Skewis might find tough today.

The manager of the chemist's shop saw no difficulty in one of his staff having a quiet chat with the police about a possible motoring offence. 'We have a little private room, Inspector, for customers who want to discuss their medication away from other customers,' he fluted with practised ease, glad to have the police out of public sight too. 'Not everyone wants to talk about their illnesses in a crowded shop.'

Detective Inspector Sloan couldn't have agreed with him more. He himself worried that he might have an incipient bunion on his left foot after his years on the beat but wild horses wouldn't have made him take his sock off in front of strangers.

Trevor Skewis, summoned by the manager, duly appeared in the discreet side room. He looked from one policeman to the other and said, 'What now?'

'We would like to know where you were yesterday evening, sir,' began Sloan. The young man's face was vaguely familiar to him although he couldn't immediately place where and when he'd seen him before. Deciding that it must have been at the Tridgell funeral, he dismissed the thought.

'Me? Whatever for?' Skewis reared up like a nervous filly.

'We ask the questions,' said Crosby importantly.

Skewis stared at him. 'And I'm supposed to answer them, am I? Without knowing why.'

'Yes,' replied that young scion of proper policing.

Detective Inspector Sloan intervened to explain. 'We are making enquiries into a road traffic accident last night at Friar's Flensant.'

Trevor Skewis relaxed at this and sat back in the customer's chair. He said, 'Well, it wasn't me.' He looked from one policeman to the other. 'I know what this is,' he then continued coldly, 'you're trying to fit me up after that other accident. I always knew you'd try to catch me on some trumped-up charge one day.'

'No,' said Sloan patiently, 'that is not the case.'

'So why the questions then?'

'Two pedestrians were knocked over not far from the Lamb and Flag Inn.'

'Nice pub,' remarked Skewis. 'They did us very well there after Paul's father's funeral.'

'Paul Tridgell was one of those knocked over,' said Sloan, ignoring this. 'His sister ended up on the ground too.'

Trevor Skewis whistled. 'So that's what this is all about.'

'Yes,' said Crosby simply.

'The encounter of man and metal presumably causing some damage to the car's front nearside wing,' supplemented Sloan. As he explained to Crosby afterwards Edmond Locard's exchange principle usually came into its own sooner or later.

Trevor Skewis's brow cleared. 'And I took my car into a garage to have my front wing repaired this morning, didn't I?'

'We know that,' said Crosby complacently.

'Silly me,' said Trevor Skewis.

'So?' said Sloan, looking interrogatively at Skewis.

'So I caught it on our gatepost going home last night,' he said defensively.

'Having had a drink?'

Skewis winced visibly, a look of pain flitting across his face. 'No, I don't drink any more these days.'

'So why the bashed wing?' asked Crosby directly.

'So why the police?' countered Skewis. 'It happened in my dad's drive, not on a public road.'

Sloan could see the words 'Sez you' forming on Crosby's lips and so before they were out of his mouth he said swiftly to Skewis, 'Where were you yesterday evening?'

'At a friend's house.'

'When did you get home?'

'About half past nine. We – that is, I – don't do late nights these days.'

'Pull the other one,' said Crosby, this time getting the words out before he could be diverted.

Detective Inspector Sloan pushed his notebook firmly forward. 'Can we please have the name and address of the friend with whom you said you spent the evening?'

'Not unless you charge me with something,' said Skewis sturdily.

At his most formal, Sloan said, 'I must remind you that obstructing the police in the course of their enquiries can constitute a serious offence.'

There was a long pause and then Trevor Skewis said suddenly, 'You won't worry her, will you? She's gone through so much.'

Then it came to Sloan. He had the policeman's trained memory for faces and remembered now where it was he had seen Trevor Skewis before. He was the man who had slipped so unobtrusively out of Elizabeth Shelford's house as he and Crosby had arrived there.

CHAPTER SIXTEEN

'Where to now, sir?' asked Crosby as they left the chemist's premises and a still militant Trevor Skewis.

Sloan read out an address from his notebook. 'The Almstone Towers Hotel, Crosby. We need to see the last man known to be both at the funeral and in that car accident and, if you remember, Tim Cullen is an under-manager there.'

'I'd forgotten him,' admitted Crosby. 'Still, there were rather a lot of them in that smash.'

'Too many,' agreed Sloan gravely, adding, 'And while we're out there at Almstone we'll take a look at Trevor Skewis's father's gatepost in Larking.'

Enjoying as ever a trip out into the countryside, Crosby soon swept the unmarked police car up to the front of a very grand hotel indeed. Too over-awed to come to a halt with his usual flourish, instead the constable brought the car to a gentle sliding halt in front of a colonnaded entrance lined with bay trees in green wooden tubs, a striped green and white awning stretching out before it. He switched off the engine and started to open the driver's door but, struck by a sudden misgiving, he stilled the action.

'What is it?' asked Sloan.

'Ought we to have gone round the back, sir?' he asked anxiously.

'To the servants' entrance, you mean? I wonder, Crosby.' Detective Inspector Sloan, eyebrows raised, shot the constable a quizzical glance and said, 'We are, of course, undoubtedly servants of the public...'

The constable sank back into the driver's seat and put his hand on the car's starter just as a uniformed minion opened the front door of the hotel and came out towards them.

'On the other hand,' went on Sloan bracingly, 'we represent law and order and there's nothing backstairs about that. Come along, Crosby, the front door. We are warranted officers of the Crown and you should never ever forget it.'

It was the minion, wearing a black waistcoat edged in green, who opened the inspector's door. 'Welcome to the Almstone Towers Hotel, sir. Would there be any luggage?'

Afraid that Crosby might be mistaken for his chauffeur, Sloan said hastily, 'No, thank you. We're not residents.'

Crosby clambered out of the driving seat and stood at a respectful distance behind Sloan.

'Then come this way please, gentlemen.' He led the way through the generous portico and escorted them to a polished walnut desk in the marbled entrance hall. This was presided over by a receptionist of so sophisticated an appearance as guaranteed to pierce the *amour-propre* of any but the most self-confident arrival. She arched her eyebrows when Sloan asked to speak to Tim Cullen but all she did was reach for a hand microphone and announce over it that Mr Cullen was wanted at reception.

A young man, soberly dressed according to the requirements of an aspirant employee of a five-star hotel, appeared without delay. When Sloan said that they wanted a word with him he swiftly led the way across a vast entrance hall to some chairs in a secluded corner, skirting a great copper tub in which rested the largest floral display Sloan had ever seen. Since the flowers were all hothouse ones, Sloan, a hardy plant gardener if ever there was one, gave them only a cursory glance. Costly blooms were not for him.

'We're police officers...' started Detective Inspector Sloan, once established in an Empire style chair and taking breath.

'I know,' interrupted Tim Cullen.

Crosby bristled. 'How?'

'Your shoes,' explained Cullen. 'In this job you learn about shoes early on.'

While Detective Constable Crosby stared down at his own pair, Tim Cullen went on, 'Besides, I saw you both at that funeral the other day. Paul Tridgell's dad's. Checking on some funny business, were you?'

'What makes you say that?' asked Sloan at once.

'Well, you wouldn't have been there otherwise, would you? Stands to reason.' He sniffed. 'I can't imagine it's because of Paul's dad having done anything he shouldn't for you to be at his funeral – he wasn't that sort of a man – so it must have been someone else.'

'Really?' The settled view of Detective Inspector Sloan was that in the first instance in an investigation any information might be useful. It was usually too soon to say whether this particular piece was helpful or not.

'Sure,' said Cullen. 'Paul's dad was a good guy. Did you know that he gave Paul the money for that trip out to Brazil? Made him promise not to tell his mum that he had, though.'

'Why not?' asked Crosby, who was not married.

Tim Cullen stared at him. 'Work it out for yourself, mate.'

Detective Inspector Sloan, who was married, made a mental note. He thought he could work it out all right.

'Besides,' went on Cullen, 'you didn't even know his dad. It was Paul who told us that about Brazil, not him. Until that stupid sister of his sent for you the police had never been in the house.' A cloud passed over his face. 'Except after the accident, of course. I expect they went round then.'

'I think you may be mistaken about the nature of our enquiries,' said Sloan, starting again. 'We are seeking information about a road traffic accident last night.'

'Not guilty,' responded Tim Cullen promptly. 'Haven't got a car any more.'

'Over at Friar's Flensant.'

'Like I said, not guilty. I use a bus and a bicycle these days. Or walk.'

'Why?' asked Crosby simply.

A shadow passed over Cullen's face again. 'Driving's not much fun any more. I didn't enjoy it at all after the smash.' He waved an arm to encompass the building they were in. 'Besides, the job here's residential.'

'What exactly do you do?' asked Crosby, clearly fascinated by his surroundings.

'In the business they call it being a *cadre stagiaire*,' Cullen sniffed, 'but if you ask me it's a posh name for being a dogsbody.'

The detective constable nodded, exuding fellow feeling. 'Somebody has to do it,' he said.

Detective Inspector Sloan got back to the business in hand. 'So someone will presumably be able to vouch for your being here all last evening.' It was a statement by the policeman, not a question.

'I'll say. They watch you like hawks at the Almstone Towers and call it training,' said Cullen bitterly. 'It's unsocial hours, too. I worked all yesterday evening and the manager was around until I went off duty.'

'And when would that have been?' asked Sloan.

'Midnight,' said Cullen. 'And the blighter sees to it that it's not a minute before. Doesn't miss a blooming thing.' He looked curiously at the two policemen. 'That lets me off the hook, does it?'

'Paul Tridgell and his sister, Jane, were knocked down last night by a hit-and-run driver on their way home from the Lamb and Flag,' said Sloan.

'Ah, so that's the name of the game, is it?' said Tim Cullen, relaxing back in his chair and looking at them both. It was impossible to tell if he was surprised by the news or not.

'The driver didn't stop,' amplified Crosby.

'Well, he wouldn't, would he?' said Cullen unexpectedly. 'I mean, if he meant to do it.'

'We don't think it was an accident either,' agreed Detective Inspector Sloan, getting up to go. 'If you have any idea who it might have been at the wheel, would you let us know?'

'Sure,' said Tim Cullen at once.

'Or know of anyone with a bashed nearside wing,' added Crosby.

'That too,' promised Cullen.

'Or know why someone would want to knock Paul Tridgell to the ground and drive on,' added Sloan for good measure. 'Perhaps you know that already and could tell us?'

But Tim Cullen made no answer to this rather different question, deferentially accompanying the two policemen to the hotel door without saying anything more at all.

In law, silence could be taken for consent. As far as Sloan was concerned, this didn't apply in detection. Nor, either, come to that, in his opinion did the continued reiteration of the words 'No Comment' amount to consent. He deemed that response to be the same as silence – an unwillingness to put anything into speech that could be examined, quoted, and re-examined afterwards. By either side, he reminded himself. Something from Kipling's poem *'If'* drifted into his mind: 'If you can bear to hear the truth you've spoken! Twisted by knaves to make a trap for fools...' In his book that went for prosecution and defence.

But Tim Cullen didn't say another word as he accompanied the two policemen to the doors of the hotel, instead politely bowing them out after the manner born as they stepped back out under the colonnade and walked towards their car between the bay trees in their little green wooden tubs.

In Sloan's view Tim Cullen might really not know who had knocked Paul Tridgell and his sister down, but on the other hand he certainly gave all the signs of having a very good idea of who the driver might have been.

Trevor Skewis's parents' house was on the farther side of the village of Larking, the downside. Armed with its address, Crosby drove the police car down one of the small streets well beyond the church, bringing the car to a halt outside a post-war semi-detached building of little architectural merit. More to the point it had a narrow drive, flanked by a pair of brick gateposts.

Both policemen got out of the car to examine these. The left-hand one bore distinct signs of having been hit by something about two feet above ground level. These signs included some flakes of black paint. Chips of broken brick were clearly visible on the ground, too.

'He's not much of a driver,' said Crosby patronisingly.

'Although,' he conceded, 'if he was coming in from the nearside in the dark, it would have been a tight turn.'

'If he hit it himself with his own car to fool us,' observed Sloan, 'then he remembered to make sure that the flakes of paint stuck to the brickwork.' He peered at the gatepost closely. 'And not with glue.'

He decided he would get Inspector Harpe's traffic team to confirm that the paint on the gatepost and the paint on Trevor Skewis's car matched. It was what their forensic friends did very well and since Superintendent Leeyes was hot on having every detail of an investigation checked out it would do no harm. That there didn't appear to be anything else that could be checked forensically Sloan knew only too well, even if the superintendent didn't.

So far, that is.

As Crosby drove back into the police station yard Detective Inspector Sloan put up his hand to stop the constable leaving the car. 'There are a few more jobs for you to get going on, Crosby, while I start writing up my report.'

'Sir?'

'First of all, you can check exactly what time it was that Trevor Skewis left Elizabeth Shelford's house last night. He says half past nine – see what she says.'

'They'll have colluded already, sir,' he pointed out reasonably enough.

'Very probably but you need to be able to tell that for sure. Listen carefully to what she says. And how.'

'Yes, sir.'

'And you can also go over to Luston and check up on the head honcho at Luston Chemicals – him with the Rolls-Royce...'

Crosby brightened. 'A Roller?'

'Don't you remember Tod telling us that he turned up at Michael Linane's funeral in it?'

'No, sir.'

'Pity, that. A good memory makes a good policeman.'

'Yes, sir. Sorry, sir.'

'And while you're about it you might as well check up on Simon Thornycroft's car, too. Best to be on the safe side.' He didn't explain that the safe side he wanted to be on was one that could not be open to any accusation of neglect by Superintendent Leeyes. His superior officer expected every avenue to be fully explored and said so. Often.

'Yes, sir.' Crosby obediently made a note.

'But leave Jonathon Sharp out of the picture for the time being. I'm waiting until I've had a phone call about him before we interview him again.'

Sloan watched the constable drive out of the police car park and then retreated to his own office, confident that these three simple – but distant – tasks would ensure that Crosby was out of his hair for long enough for he himself to sit back quietly and consider the problem.

Cradling his hands round a large mug of tea at his desk, Sloan did just that. His wife, Margaret, called it being 'thinkative'. When he protested that this wasn't a word, she only smiled and said it was now. He would have been hard put to put into words what he was hoping to come to mind when he sat there but he always thought of doing so as a sort of mental 'alpenglow'. The alpenglow was something he had seen on his first never-to-be-forgotten trip to Switzerland – a rosy hue, back-lighting the mountains long after the sun had gone down.

That's what he needed now – just that same latent illumination, throwing a special extra light on what he had gleaned so far just when the darkness all around was deepening.

Setting down his mug of tea, he drew his note-book towards him and, as he had been taught, started again at the beginning. It had all seemed quite simple to start with: a patient had died of undoubtedly natural causes – the doctor had confirmed that – but using his last breath to accuse another man of a killing. Sloan was human enough to wish that that accusation had been just a little bit more specific but it hadn't been and that was all there was to it.

Except, of course, that it wasn't all there was to it. There was also the fact that the man's son, Paul Tridgell, would appear to know who had done the killing – and in Sloan's opinion had been unwise

168

enough to make this obvious at his father's funeral. And there was now also the fact that last night someone unknown had tried to mow him down: someone unknown to the police, that is, but not to Paul Tridgell, if that young man's demeanour was anything to go on. He would dearly have liked to know why he was keeping silent.

And, perhaps, known to Tim Cullen, too. That is, if that other young man's dedicated silence was anything to go on. It was difficult to say.

He wasn't sure either about Trevor Skewis and his attentive relationship with the half-paralysed Elizabeth Shelford. Did guilt come into that, he asked himself, but answer came there none. The young man said he had left her side early enough to have got to the pub in Friar's Flensant at the right time. And his car had a damaged nearside front wing.

And he still didn't know where someone called the wrong remainderman came into the picture.

If he did, that is.

Sloan took another mouthful of tea and decided that the police now had two quite separate aims – to find out who had killed whom and to avert any attempt by whoever it was also to kill Paul Tridgell. He immediately scribbled down another objective that had also occurred to him – to stop the aforementioned Paul Tridgell proceeding with his own investigations – and perhaps, exacting revenge – all on his own. Keeping that tiresome young man out of harm's way was going to be quite a problem.

Otherwise it seemed to him to be not so much a three pipe problem as a three possibilities problem – unfortunately it was the precise nature of the problem that was not yet obvious. That there had been three involvements with death by the late Derek Tridgell was not in question. Admittedly he hadn't been present at that fatal road accident last Christmas but it wasn't unreasonable for him to be concerned as his son had been one of those involved in that murky and unresolved event. Moreover, that same young man had taken off for foreign parts almost immediately afterwards – and, it would seem – with his father's sub rosa financial help.

Sloan pulled his thoughts up with a jerk. Flight – even when it was assisted – was not automatically a sign of guilt and like all right-thinking policemen he must remember that. Nevertheless he knew many a father would gladly pay to save a son from a long prison sentence.

Then there was the dreadful death of Michael Linane over at Luston Chemicals. A tragic accident, according to the relevant authorities after a full investigation but, coincidence or not, Derek Tridgell had been in their chemical works on the day with his boss, Jonathon Sharp, both with time unaccounted for. And on a failed mission that had involved Michael Linane.

And although Ralph Iddon, Chairman of that firm, had not been at the funeral to see Derek Tridgell's son's unmistakeable emphasis on the word 'kill' in his reading at the church, Jonathon Sharp had definitely been there. Simon Thornycroft, he remembered, had actually nodded in Sharp's direction when he mentioned him in his eulogy, something that Sloan had seen for himself.

He had already been determined to have yet

another chat with Jonathon Sharp, the chairman of Berebury Pharmaceuticals. After all, he was a man who after Derek Tridgell's death had not scrupled to poach a former employee from his deadly rival, Luston Chemicals. That was why he was now waiting for a telephone call from the City of London.

And the dead man, Michael Linane, Head of Sales, must have been a thorn in the flesh of the manufacturer of Ameliorite, Sharp's firm, in fact just as much a threat as Ralph Iddon was. Predatory pricing might be illegal but it was a commercial crime and would take its time to work its way through the courts, much too late to stop the rot in the losing side. It wasn't cricket either but then he knew already that business was not cricket. Everybody did. He would have to think about this. Cricket and illegality were two different things – just like sin and crime – and he would have to remember that, too.

There was that other death involving Derek Tridgell, which had also been deemed to have been accidental – with more cause perhaps than the one at the chemical works. That was the roof fall in the Chislet Crags and the subsequent death of Edmund Leaton. For the life of him, Sloan couldn't think of that as a deliberate killing – more bad luck or fate, whichever of the two you believed in. But Derek Tridgell had been there then, too, and he mustn't forget that.

Mentally he had already categorised caving as on the list of those dangerous sports likely to cause the constabulary unnecessary work. Racing fast cars faster and faster was another of them.

171

Dicing with death was not his own idea of fun and he was already mentally rehearsing good reasons for not allowing his infant son to have a motorcycle in the years to come.

With no positive action still ahead, he sat back for a moment, nevertheless dissatisfied with his lack of any conclusions from his thinking, although somewhere at the back of his mind he was aware of a small inconsistency – something that didn't quite tie up. It was niggling away but he couldn't bring it to mind. He sat quite still, willing it to come to him but, try as he might, he couldn't put his finger on it.

As he set his empty mug down, it did come to him exactly what was so conspicuously lacking in this case: there was no scene of crime to be inspected and thus start the police on a trail to a killer.

And no remains to be seen either.

Which was even less helpful.

CHAPTER SEVENTEEN

The next visitor to arrive at Legate Lodge in Friar's Flensant that morning clearly felt no need to stand on ceremony. True, she did ring the doorbell first but she opened the front door without waiting for it to be answered, calling out as she did so, 'Cooee, anyone at home? Can I come in?'

The new arrival was tall and had auburn hair

172

that was set off to perfection by a cream scarf and light brown coat. She was startlingly good-looking in a timeless way, with the almost translucent complexion that often goes with auburn hair. She was one of those fortunate women who could easily stay at a declared age of thirty-nine for another decade.

Marion Tridgell welcomed her with open arms. 'Come along in, Amelia, and I'll put some coffee on. It's lovely to see you.'

'I thought it was high time I came to see you all,' said Amelia Thornycroft, pulling off the scarf and settling herself down comfortably at the kitchen table. 'And see how you are all getting along.'

Marion Tridgell, having switched on the coffee percolator, pulled up a chair opposite her and unburdened herself to her friend. 'Have you heard about our latest excitement? If that's the right way to describe it.' She winced. 'I'm not sure that it is.'

Amelia Thornycroft shook her head and said, 'Tell me.'

'Someone tried to run Paul and Jane down last night on their way home from the pub.'

'No! Not on purpose, surely?'

'Paul says so.'

'Never!' She put out a hand to Marion. 'You poor dear – I would have thought you'd have had quite enough to contend with this year already.'

'I have,' responded Marion wearily. 'But this was a bit different. And unexpected.' She recounted the events of the night before to her friend to the accompaniment of increasingly loud thumps from the coffee percolator.

Amelia Thornycroft opened her blue eyes wide.

'I can't really believe it.'

'I'm not sure that I can either, but the police think it wasn't an accident.' Nobody was going to underestimate Marion Tridgell's age today. On the contrary. Last night's events had visibly aged her.

'A hit-and-run, you mean?'

'No,' said Marion Tridgell. 'I do mean on purpose.'

'My dear, how awful. Who could do a thing like that? And why on earth would they want to anyway?'

'I can't begin to imagine. Oh, Amelia, I can't even think straight about it all.'

'Oh, dear. The poor lambs. And how are they? The children, I mean.'

'Jane's quite upset and very quiet and Paul...' she paused. 'I'm not sure about Paul. He seems more cross than anything. And he's not saying much either.'

Amelia smiled, emphasising the laughter lines on her face. 'Keeping quiet? That doesn't sound like the Paul whom we all know and love.'

This elicited something like a smile at last from Marion. 'It's not the only thing that's worrying me, Amelia. Now he's quite determined to go caving like his father.' Mentioning her late husband by name was a stage in her bereavement journey that had yet to be reached.

'Paul?' Amelia raised her delicately arched eyebrows. 'I thought he didn't like the sport, if a sport is what it is. I'm never sure about that.'

'I call it a madness,' said Marion trenchantly. 'I always did.'

'Don't you remember Derek trying to interest

174

him in it ages ago? And him saying "not likely" or improper words to that effect.'

'I do,' Paul's mother said. 'That's what's so strange about him wanting to take it up now.'

A shadow crossed Amelia Thornycroft's face. 'He knows what happened to my poor Edmund down that awful cave, doesn't he?'

Marion nodded sympathetically. 'He does. His father explained it to him at the time, although he was much younger then.'

'Seven years is a long time at that age.' She sighed. 'Not when you're older, though. It still seems like yesterday that Edmund died. Lucy was only three and I don't think she really remembers him. Or if she does, it's all a bit of a blur now.' Deftly, she changed the subject. 'Actually, Marion, strictly between ourselves, Lucy's getting a bit difficult these days.'

'She's beginning to grow up, that's all, Amelia. Children do.'

'I know, but she will call Simon her *faux pas*. Oh, I know it's quite clever but I'm not sure he really likes it. It was all my fault, too.' She brushed her hair back from her forehead. 'Do you remember when I had that lovely hat? The imitation fur one?'

'Of course, I do.' She smiled. 'You looked great in it. It really suited you.'

'Well, Lucy asked me what sort of animal the fur had come from – you know how they all go through that saving animals phase – so I explained that it wasn't real fur but false and that was what *"faux"* meant.'

'Which it does, of course.'

'Exactly. Then she heard the expression *"faux*

175

pas" somewhere else and put two and two together.'

'And made five,' said Marion sympathetically.

'And Simon just thinks she's calling him a
mistake.'

'The other sort of *faux pas*,' agreed Marion.
'The sort of mistake you hope you never make in
public.'

Amelia Thornycroft frowned. 'I must remember
to tell Simon about the hat and how the name
came about.'

'It must always be difficult, being a step-parent,'
said Marion, switching off the percolator and
bringing two mugs over to the table. She soon got
back to what was really worrying her. 'Kate Booth
has been teaching Paul the ropes. About caving, I
mean. Abseiling, that sort of thing.'

'Dear Kate,' Amelia said absently. 'Simon says
she's a great caver. What is it he calls her? A real
rock chick, that's it.'

'And there's all his father's caving tackle still here
in the garage,' persisted Marion. 'He wouldn't let
me give it away when he got ill.' It was Marion's
turn to let a shadow cross her face. 'Oh, Amelia,
we are a great pair of lookers-back, aren't we?'

Amelia Thornycroft brushed a tear away from
the corner of her eye and said quietly, 'I think we
should both be grateful that we've got good
things to look back on, that's all.'

Marion Tridgell nodded, tacitly agreeing with
her. 'The past is safe. Nobody can change that.
It's the future I'm so concerned about. Last night
was no accident. Paul is quite sure about that and
I know him well enough to believe him, but he's

not saying anything like enough about it to anyone – least of all the police – for my liking.'

Amelia stared at her friend. 'You mean you
think he knows who was driving?'

'I'm very much afraid so – I know what he's
like, you see. Oh, Amelia,' she said with taut lips,
'I'm so worried about him.'

'I'm not surprised.' Amelia picked up her mug,
draining the last of her coffee. As she set it back
on the kitchen table she said, 'Can I see Jane and
Paul before I go? I don't like the sound of what's
happened one little bit.'

Given three assignments, one of which included
seeing a Rolls-Royce, there was no contest in
Detective Constable Crosby's mind as to where he
should go first, whatever his orders. He made his
way to Luston Chemicals and drew up at the
entrance to the car park. An attendant appeared at
his side as if by magic and asked him his business.

Crosby flashed his warrant card in front of the
man. 'I'd like to examine the boss's car, please,'
he said.

'Not without the boss's say-so,' responded the
man. He was chewing gum. 'You'll have to ask
him first.'

'As much as your job's worth, I suppose,' par-
roted Crosby.

'Too right, mate. What's he gone and done now,
then?' he asked.

'That's not for me to say,' said Crosby austerely.

'You'll be lucky to catch him at it, whatever it
is,' said the man complacently. 'Clever chap is

177

our Ralph Iddon. Very.'

'It's his car I want to see, not him.'

'Which one? He's got two.'

'Both of them, then. What are they?'

'A Roller for high days and holidays and a runabout for everyday.'

'And which one did he go home in last night?'

The man waved his hand round the large open parking lot. 'Which do you think, mate? Would you leave that much money all on its lonesome here overnight?'

'No,' said Crosby, who chained his own bicycle up to the nearest stanchion, day or night. He looked round. 'So where is it now, then?'

He sniffed. 'Standing outside the front door of the works to impress the natives as usual, I expect.'

'And the runabout?'

The man indicated a small car, tucked neatly into a nearby parking bay. Crosby photographed it, then examined it carefully without finding any evidence of its having had an impact with anything untoward.

'And what time did Mr Iddon leave here yesterday?' he asked.

The man scratched his head. 'He knocked off early, being the boss. About four, I would say.'

'Some people have all the luck.' Police hours were a sore subject with Crosby, who was only just getting used to the fact that they were seldom only from nine to five on weekdays.

'Mind you,' conceded the man, 'he's an early bird. I will say that for him.'

'Catches the worm, does he?' said Crosby, his attention caught by a motorist nosing around the

178

crowded car park for somewhere to leave his vehicle. There was one vacant space quite near the entrance but the driver didn't attempt to enter it. Instead he went on driving around looking for another one. Crosby pointed to the space. 'That's reserved for the Roller, is it?'

The man shook his head. 'No, that's the place that was reserved for the car of the late Michael Linane, our old head of sales. Nobody wants to be the first to use it since he died. And so they don't.'

Crosby leafed through his memory. 'The poor guy who ended up in a vat of the nasty stuff?'

'That was him.'

'Funny business, that,' offered Crosby.

'I'll say, especially as two blokes from another firm were here at the time – and they had it in for him, big time. If you ask me...' He stopped.

'Yes?'

'They didn't get to the bottom of it. They tried, all right. Place was swarming with health and safety people at the time and now they've all come back again all this time after.'

'Why?' asked Crosby.

'Didn't do the job properly the first time, I expect. You know what they're like.'

'Go on.'

But the man wouldn't say anything more even when Crosby asked about another vacancy in the firm.

'Which was that then?' asked the car park man.

'Your chief chemist, Chris Honley,' said Crosby, a name coming back to him.

'Oh, him.' The man aimed some chewing gum at the floor. 'That rat.'

'Left a sinking ship, has he?' suggested Crosby provocatively.

'Certainly not. We're doing all right here, we are.'

'So where's his old parking space, then?'

'Filled immediately,' said the man, spitting out the residue of his chewing gum in a meaningful way.

The time spent by Crosby examining the Rolls-Royce was more of a tribute to the car than police business. So was his photograph.

'Lovely, isn't she?' said Ralph Iddon. 'You can't beat the best.' They were standing outside the front of Luston Chemicals.

'Not bad,' pronounced Detective Constable Crosby. 'Not bad at all.'

Taking this as high praise, Iddon opened the driver's door. 'Like to sit in it?'

'You bet, sir,' said Crosby. He had already taken a good look at the left-hand nearside of the vehicle and had seen not a single scratch or dent in it. 'Just as a matter of form, sir, can you tell me where you were last night?'

The chairman of Luston Chemicals gave the constable a very straight look and said without hesitation, 'In the town hall speaking to the Luston Chamber of Trade about the parlous condition of today's manufacturing industry.' He pursed his lips and said drily, 'If it's an alibi you're after I daresay enough of the audience were still awake to give me one.'

'I'm sure that won't be necessary, sir, thank you,' said Crosby, reluctantly clambering out of the car. 'Just a routine enquiry.'

'About something that wasn't routine, though, I daresay,' deduced the other man without difficulty. 'And I suppose you are going to say now that you can't tell me exactly what.'

'Yes, sir. I am. I mean, I can't.' He fell back on another well-honed phrase. 'Not until all our enquiries are complete.'

CHAPTER EIGHTEEN

The great disadvantage of Detective Inspector Sloan's office as a place for deep thought – or even simple contemplation – was soon made manifest by the buzz of the telephone disturbing his concentration.

'That you, Sloan?' At the other end of the line was Superintendent Leeyes summoning him to his office. Sloan put his notes into a neat pile on his desk and duly presented himself in front of his superior officer, trying to look attentive.

'What's all this about a road traffic accident at Friar's Flensant last night?' asked that luminary, pulling the open folder that lay on his desk towards him and staring at a report.

'We don't think it was an accident and neither does Paul Tridgell,' said Sloan.

'Like that, is it?' scowled the superintendent.

'A hit-and-run,' amplified Sloan, 'but not an accident.'

'And, pray, may I ask, does that help or hinder your enquiries?'

'It gives some substance to them,' said Sloan guardedly.

'What I would really like, Sloan,' said Leeyes, 'is a progress report on the whole Tridgell affair. Soon.'

'Yes, sir,' began Sloan.

'And,' he added testily, 'I don't just want a bleat about the present state of play.'

'No, sir.'

'Or that you're planning to do something useful next either. I want to know exactly what you've found out so far. Only the facts, please, Sloan.' He sniffed. 'Speculation should come after the facts, not before, remember.'

Detective Inspector Sloan took a deep breath and plunged into speech. 'Not a lot of them to go on yet, I'm afraid, sir,' he admitted. 'The deceased – Derek Tridgell – was present at one death – the one in the cave – and might – we don't know for certain – have been present at another – the drowning of a man in a vat of undisclosed contents.'

'Not malmsey, anyway,' pronounced Leeyes.

'Beg pardon, sir?'

'It was how they did for the Duke of Clarence,' said Leeyes simply.

'The pub in Staple St James?' said Sloan, thoroughly confused. 'Never any trouble there to speak of, sir. Not that I've heard, anyway. The publican had been in the army. Sergeant, I think. Big chap, not to be trifled with.'

'No, no, not him. The brother of King Richard III,' said Leeyes. 'He was drowned in a butt of the stuff.'

182

Sloan searched his mind and then it came to him. That must have come not from a well-run public house out in the country named after a Duke of Clarence but from a course on the later Plantagenets once attended by the superintendent. It had been a brief encounter, the superintendent taking the view that any half-decent police investigation would have very soon established beyond doubt whom it was who had been responsible for the deaths of the two little princes in the Tower, means, motive and opportunity in his view all being present in abundance. What had been missing, in his view, was justice.

Sloan hurried on. 'Derek Tridgell's connection with the third death is only tangential, sir, since it involved his son, not him, but he is said to have facilitated the son's going to South America quite soon after being involved in an unresolved fatal road traffic accident.'

The superintendent perked up immediately and looked quite cheerful for once. 'Extradition's a lot easier from there these days than it used to be, Sloan.'

'No warrant was issued after the accident, sir.' Sloan shook his head. 'Unfortunately it couldn't be established who to serve it on.'

Leeyes sniffed. 'One of those safety in numbers cop-outs, I suppose.' The superintendent reserved his severest condemnation for judges who, unable to properly apportion guilt between two defendants, sentenced neither.

'In a manner of speaking,' said Sloan warily. He wasn't entirely sure if not disclosing the name of the driver in the fatal car crash – if it was really known, that is – could be construed as obstructing the police in the course of their enquiries or not, and therefore be chargeable. One thing he was quite sure about though was that the patently obvious alliance of the survivors of the crash might not be as cast-iron as they wanted the police to think. Not now that someone had taken a potshot so to speak at Paul Tridgell who was one of their number. He cheered up slightly himself. Accidents that weren't accidents were the very stuff of police investigations.

'I still say it's a cop-out,' insisted Leeyes trenchantly.

'Quite so, sir. In theory, of course, the father could have had a vested interest in sheltering his son from prosecution.' He didn't add that now the police wanted to save Paul from something much worse. 'But only in theory.'

'So?'

At last Sloan got back to the point he wanted to make. 'However, whatever Derek Tridgell knew, he had obviously been prepared to live with it for quite a while before he died which is very interesting.'

'Until he was too near death to keep quiet any longer,' agreed the superintendent.

'They say confession is good for the soul, sir,' murmured Sloan. His own mother, a noted churchwoman, always insisted on this being so. 'Myself, I wouldn't know.'

'It clears up crime quicker than anything else we can do,' said the superintendent, a pragmatist if ever there was one.

'What occurred to me as really odd, sir,'

184

persisted Sloan, 'is that the killing, or whatever else it was, didn't seem to have made all that much difference to everyone in Derek Tridgell's circle at the time.'

'Or,' pointed out Superintendent Leeyes, immediately putting his finger on a weakness in Sloan's argument, 'the man had something to lose by disclosing what he knew.'

Detective Inspector Sloan nodded. 'That might well be the case, sir. One of the people in the building at Luston when Michael Linane fell into that vat was Tridgell's own boss, Jonathon Sharp. I can quite understand that Tridgell might have had a vested interest in not shopping him if he had done something wrong. He'd have lost his job. Only if it was him, of course,' he added belatedly.

'Or Big Pharma might have been ready to make it worthwhile to button lips,' said Leeyes cynically. 'You never know with businesses of that size.'

'Very true, sir,' agreed Sloan, although he didn't know a lot about big business. What he did know about it, though, he didn't particularly like.

'There's a lot to be said,' pronounced Leeyes, a man well known for toadying to the higher ranks in the force in the interests of his own career, 'for knowing on which side your bread is buttered.'

'There's something else I've been thinking about, sir,' said Sloan.

'Get on with it then, man. I haven't got all day.'

'I'm not quite sure how to put it, sir,' began Sloan. There had been something in a lecture on legal history he had heard in his training that had surfaced in his mind since he'd been caught up

185

with what he had – perforce – called the Tridgell case. It had been a brief lecture, cantering smartly from the Bow Street Runners through to today's forensic scientists, via Jonathan Wild and Sir Robert Peel. Some of it, though, had stuck in his memory including the fact that once upon a time murder had been deemed to be not a crime per se but more simply as a disturbance of the Queen's peace. Until some Victorian Act of Parliament changed its designation to that of the more straightforward crime of homicide, the Queen's peace was said to have been restored only when the culprit had been caught and justice done.

And what was interesting, Sloan said now, was that there hadn't been any noticeable disturbance of the Queen's peace by any death connected with the late Derek Tridgell. It didn't appear to have upset any pre-existing applecart either, which was equally strange. He listed the deaths for the super-intendent.

Michael Linane, one-time Head of Sales at Luston Chemicals, had been decently buried after a full inquest and quietly replaced. Only those officials concerned with health and safety at work seemed still interested in his fatal accident. Or so Crosby had reported.

Edmund Leaton's body was still entombed underground by falling rock but someone else was – in the poet's words – now seeing his wife and child fed.

And whomsoever had been at the wheel of the car on the night of the fatal road traffic accident was still going about their lawful business. That, of course, didn't include Elizabeth Shelford who wasn't going very far at all in her wheelchair, but who was being conspicuously well supported by three out of four of her surviving fellow passengers.

Superintendent Leeyes started to tap the file on his desk with his pencil. 'As scenes of crime go, Sloan, I must say they don't amount to very much.'

'No, sir, though Crosby's still checking on two or three more vehicles that might have hit young Tridgell and his sister last night.'

'Someone was warning the boy off, I suppose,' grunted Leeyes.

'We think so, sir, which is very worrying.' He added a rider. 'Or perhaps trying to put him out of action.'

'Downright dangerous, if you ask me,' said Leeyes unhelpfully. 'Right, that's all for now, Sloan, but don't let anything else happen to him.'

'No, sir,' sighed Sloan. Like most of the superintendent's instructions this was not going to be easy to accomplish.

'And Sloan...'

Sloan paused at the door. 'Sir?'

'Don't forget,' said the superintendent enigmatically, 'that there are dangers in playing the man, not the football. Forget the deceased. He didn't do it. It's the football you should be after.'

'I won't forget, sir,' promised Sloan, making his escape from the superintendent's room without being any the wiser than he had been before he entered it. There should be a phone call coming in soon, though, which might help.

'Sorry to bother you again, miss,' began Detective Constable Crosby. He was standing on the doorstep of Laguna House, Elizabeth Shelford's house at Larking.

'It's Constable Crosby, isn't it?' the owner said, peering up at him from her wheelchair.

'That's right, miss.'

She frowned. 'I've told the police everything I can remember about the accident already. You know that.'

'Yes, miss, but this is different.'

She raised a pair of finely shaped eyebrows. 'In what way?'

'It's about last night,' he said awkwardly.

'Last night?' She stiffened visibly, her knuckles turning white where they gripped the handles of her wheelchair. 'What about last night? Tell me quickly. Has something else happened?'

'Only in a manner of speaking, miss. We just want to know if you had visitors.'

The young woman looked him up and down and then said, 'You'd better come in.' She spun the wheelchair round with practised ease and led the way to the kitchen. 'Now sit down and tell me what this is all about.'

'We need to know if you had any visitors last evening,' he repeated, pulling up a chair to the table and studying her properly at close quarters for the first time. He hadn't realised on his last visit quite how young and attractive Elizabeth Shelford was. She could scarcely be any older than he was and, save for having two patently useless legs, was vibrantly alive. He realised, too, how cleverly she was dressed. A cream coloured scarf spilt out over a cerise jumper which co-ordinated well with the pair of black velvet trousers she was wearing. Two black shoes with pom-poms on their toes peeped out from under the trousers and were just visible on the footrests of her wheelchair. Whatever had happened to her body, the young woman's spirit remained un-diminished. He cast an involuntary glance at his own shoes and quickly looked away again.

'What if I did?' She manoeuvred her chair expertly over to a worktop and had plugged in a kettle almost before he realised she was on the move again.

'We need to know,' he said.

'Why?'

'In the pursuit of our enquiries into a matter that has arisen,' he said falling back, like many a policeman before him, on the rubric.

'What matter?' she said tightly. 'Tell me, what's happened? Please.'

'We would just like know who your visitors were and when they left,' said the detective con-stable patiently.

'I had three,' she said unexpectedly, her back still to him.

'And their names?'

'Trevor Skewis for one.' She hesitated. 'He's all right, isn't he? I mean nothing's happened to him, has it?'

'Not that we know about, miss. And the others?'

'Paul Tridgell and Tim Cullen.' She turned and looked at him. 'So why the enquiry? Tell me.'

Crosby countered her question with one of his own. 'When did they leave you?' he asked, tugging his notebook out of his pocket.

'Paul Tridgell and Tim Cullen went quite early...'

'And Trevor Skewis?'

'Half past nine,' she said, turning her back to him again. 'He always goes by then.'

Crosby watched as a deep blush climbed up her cheeks.

'I mean, he never stays really late.' She spun her wheelchair round, turning back to the worktop again and said, 'Come over and pick up our tea.'

Crosby obediently walked over to her, collected two brimming mugs of tea and brought them back to the table. 'Steady hands,' she commented.

'Do you live alone?' he asked curiously. An infant in these matters, he had only just realised that the shade of her nail polish matched the cerise of her jumper.

'My mother comes down every morning,' she said, 'before she goes to school – she's a teacher – and some of the boys usually turn up in the evening. My father's away a lot – he works abroad.'

'The boys?'

'The others who were in the car accident with me – Paul Tridgell, Tim Cullen and Trevor Skewis. I told you about all of them before. Not Danny Saville. He isn't really one of us. The other two left early last night because Tim Cullen had to be at work and Paul was taking his sister out for a drink.'

'But Trevor Skewis stayed on?'

'That's right.' A faint blush suffused her cheeks again. 'He ... he's been very helpful since the accident.'

Crosby looked round. 'Do you get out at all

yourself, miss? I see you've got a car in the yard.' He'd noticed its adaptations, too, but thought it wouldn't be tactful to mention them.

'Just to the hospital,' she said rather shortly. 'Nowhere else.'

'So what do you do all day?' he asked curiously.

'I pick oakum, Constable. In other words, I languish.'

'This drink of Paul's last night,' said Crosby, embarrassed and swiftly getting back to business. 'Did you all know about it?'

'Oh, yes. He told us that he and Jane were going to the Lamb and Flag pub at Friar's Flensant – it's their local, you might say.'

Detective Constable Crosby wrote something in his notebook.

'Did it matter?' asked Elizabeth Shelford.

'Oh, yes,' said Crosby and told her that someone had tried to run Paul and Jane Tridgell down on their way home from the Lamb and Flag the night before.

She sat very still, absorbing the news. 'Are you sure?'

'Paul Tridgell is,' said Crosby.

'Paul is sure about a lot of things,' she said. 'Too sure for his own good sometimes.'

'So, naturally,' he said, getting up to go, 'we're checking on everything we can.'

'Of course.' Elizabeth Shelford lowered her mug to the table. 'Go softly, Constable,' she said enigmatically, 'and you'll go further.'

CHAPTER NINETEEN

It was an unexpected crunch on the gravel outside their house that brought Amelia Thornycroft
to the sitting-room window. The sound came
from a small dusty truck that had drawn up
outside their front door. To her surprise she saw
her husband tumble out of it, wave to the driver
and make for the door of the house as it drove
away. The sound of the front door slamming
behind him alerted her to the fact that all was not
well.

Amelia, responding both to Simon's unusually
early return and the noisy entry, hurried through
into the hall. 'Whatever's happened, Simon?' she
asked. 'Are you all right?'

'I'm fine, thank you,' he said tautly.

'Where's your car, then?'

'Over in Forbes' garage, that's where,' he said
with tightened lips. 'Being repaired. They brought
me home. Damn fool of an earthmover driver on
the site backed into me first thing this morning
and hit my front wing. It's covered in yellow paint
but even so he swore he didn't see me behind
him.'

'Oh, dear,' said Amelia, exuding wifely sympathy as he came over and delivered her a kiss on
her forehead. 'But as long as neither of you was
hurt. That's what's important.' She regarded him
anxiously. 'You're not hurt, are you, Simon?'

'No, my dear, I'm not hurt.' He relaxed and gave her a little smile. 'Just in pride and pocket, I suppose.'

'Can't do anything about the pride,' she responded lightly, 'but I daresay the insurance will see to the pocket.'

'I'm not so sure about that,' he grumbled. 'Car insurance doesn't usually cover you off-road and this was on the northern bridge site which is pretty uneven and mucky anyway.'

'What about the firm?' she said. 'You're working there for them.'

'They'll be a better bet. I'll have to find out what it's going to cost first – a bomb, I expect. These vehicle repairers see you coming and they always expect it to be an insurance job even if it isn't. The other driver swore he didn't see me,' he added as an afterthought. 'More likely he wasn't looking.'

'Couldn't he hear you?'

'He had ear defenders on,' said Thornycroft absently. 'This outfit that are building the bridge are pretty keen on health and safety, you know.'

'I'm glad to hear it,' said his wife dryly.

'Besides, our car's supposed to have a quiet engine, remember?' he said, not really listening to her. 'It was quite a selling point when I bought it. No, the trouble is that these fellows will drive them too fast. They forget they're not out on the open road.'

'Where they shouldn't drive too quickly, either,' she said pertinently.

'I expect it's a dull old job from their point of view, and they're usually young,' he conceded, calming down by degrees. 'But then, to cap it all, while I was on the phone to the garage fixing up the paint job, the police turned up.'

She looked puzzled. 'Whatever for?'

'That's what I wanted to know. I thought at first some nosy parker in the office had sent for them after she'd seen the earthmover back into me – there's a sanctimonious young woman in there who takes herself altogether too seriously. She's always looking for trouble.'

'But it wasn't?' said Amelia.

'It turned out he was making enquiries about an accident last night in Friar's Flensant, although why they think it could be anything to do with me I can't imagine.'

'It was Paul Tridgell who was hit,' she informed him. 'And his sister, Jane.'

'Was it? Oh dear.' He grunted. 'Not hurt, I hope, either of them?'

'Not badly, but Paul insists they were run down on purpose,' she said, wincing.

'Ah, that explains why the police came out to see me. They know I know them both. The policeman wouldn't say, though. How did you know?'

'Marion told me when I went to see her today. I saw Paul and Jane, too. Both a bit shaken, I should say.'

'I'm not surprised.' Thornycroft frowned. 'I don't like the sound of that accident, Amelia. The Tridgell family have had quite enough to put up with as it is already.'

'I expect the police are checking up on everyone who knows him,' she said.

'Can't blame them for that,' he said. 'I don't

hold any brief for that young man but even so I wouldn't want anything like that to happen to him. I showed the policeman my car and all he could say was that if it had been as damaged as all that from hitting a pedestrian he would expect the casualty to be dead. And so would I.' Simon Thornycroft ran a hand through his hair. 'I wouldn't put it past Paul to have mentioned me to the police, all the same. And everyone else he knew.'

'Why on earth would he have done that?' asked Amelia.

'Just to be difficult,' said her husband trenchantly. 'Derek always found him a bit of a handful. Bit of a disappointment, too, that boy, and never out of trouble.'

'That's not fair,' protested Amelia. 'He's quite a nice lad really.'

'He's a bundle of trouble, my dear. His father was sorry he wouldn't take up caving when he was young, although I must say that I wasn't,' he said. 'Now it looks as if he's changed his mind because Kate Booth rang me at work yesterday and asked if she could come round here at the weekend and borrow some spare kit of mine for him.'

'It'll be nice to see her again,' said Amelia.

'I don't know how he'll cope with abseiling,' said Thornycroft pessimistically.

'I expect he will,' said Amelia.

'And never forget,' he went on, 'his father couldn't get him out of the country quickly enough after that awful road accident. The whole carload must have been drunk as skunks.' He gave a great stretch. 'Talking of drinks, I wouldn't mind one now, darling, and I'm not driving, remember.'

When Crosby got back to the police station, Detective Inspector Sloan, provincial policeman, was just coming to the end of a long telephone call with a policeman in the City of London whose remit was much wider than that of a mere division in the Calleshire County Constabulary. His beat was worldwide and related to money and one of its many illegal spin-offs, commercial fraud.

'Thank you for coming back to me,' said Sloan.

'No problem, Inspector,' said the man at the other end of the line. 'Let me see now, it was Berebury Pharmaceuticals you wanted to know all about, wasn't it?'

'That's right. A firm attacked recently by Luston Chemicals with predatory pricing.'

'There's a lot of it about,' said the money man. 'No pressure, no diamond,' he added obliquely.

'Eat or be eaten, I suppose,' observed Sloan in response.

'Nasty as well as illegal,' said the other man. 'Does a lot of damage.'

That there was no such thing as a victimless crime, Sloan knew already. And that most crimes were nasty.

'The customer likes the undercut prices, of course,' the man was going on, happily oblivious of Sloan's views. 'In the first instance, that is. They soon get to see the other side of the coin, of course, and they don't like that then.'

'Higher prices,' deduced Sloan.

'Very much higher prices,' said the other man,

'because they've effectively killed off the opposition since the market has been cornered. They can charge whatever they like as soon as they have the monopoly.'

'Berebury Pharmaceuticals would appear to have fought back by poaching Luston's chief chemist,' said Sloan tentatively.

'H'm.' There was a noticeable pause at the City end of the line. 'And they let him go without much of a struggle, you say?'

'Only gardening leave that I know about,' said Sloan. That Chris Honley had just been waiting in the wings for Derek Tridgell to die, he didn't say.

'I don't like the sound of that,' said the money man quickly. 'No great offers of raising of salary, extra bonuses, to keep him on board? Golden handcuffs? That sort of thing? On either hand? In my world, Inspector, you should always follow the money.'

'Not that I've heard,' admitted Sloan.

'Find out,' advised the man. 'You snooze, you lose. It could be important.'

'Perhaps the Berebury people offered him more money still?' suggested Sloan diffidently.

'I thought they were supposed to be on their financial knees?'

'I hadn't thought of that,' admitted Sloan humbly.

'Doesn't make sense to me,' said the man from the City. 'If you ask me he should have been the last person you'd want to invite into your outfit.'

'A Trojan horse?' That hadn't occurred to Sloan either. He must always remember that the new

197

man at Berebury Pharmaceuticals, Chris Honley, was a replacement for Derek Tridgell, deceased, he who had died accusing an unknown man of killing someone also unknown.

'Well, the new man there's going to get his hands on all the work his predecessor had in hand, isn't he? That could work both ways, of course.'

'You mean that Berebury Pharmaceuticals might have had something good in hand when their man died? Or that the Luston lot might have had something that Berebury wanted.' It made simple larceny sound positively maidenly to Sloan.

'Someone is said to have killed someone, you told me,' the City man said. 'The sort of knowledge we're talking about here can be very valuable. Work in progress, they call it. Can be really good stuff sometimes. And worth a lot.'

'Surely,' objected Sloan, 'just moving one man out of one outfit and into another couldn't make all that much difference?'

'Don't let a headhunting firm hear you say that, Inspector. It's heresy from their point of view. Their credo is that it can.'

'And does it?' he asked. Prima donnas were not encouraged in the police force. Teamwork was what got all the plaudits, definitely not an officer who, grand-standing, stood on the steps of a court and implied the conviction was all due to what he had done. That never went down well in the canteen.

'If it's a head of department man they've appointed then that man can go into every nook and cranny of the firm with impunity,' said the man in the City. 'And,' he added ominously, 'do what they like when they get there.'

'You mean...' began Sloan.

'I mean industrial espionage, Inspector,' said the money man crisply. 'Plant a cuckoo's egg in their IT system – that sort of thing. That would finish Berebury Pharmaceuticals off completely. For good and all, if that's what Luston Chemicals have in mind, which I must say I am beginning to wonder.'

Detective Inspector Sloan didn't usually feel so naïve. 'I hadn't thought of that,' he said slowly.

'On the other hand,' the man went on, warming to his theme, 'there is always the possibility that the Berebury firm had made a discovery that the Luston lot wanted. They'd have let their man go very easily to the Berebury outfit if they thought he could report back with that sort of news.'

'I hadn't thought of that either,' said Sloan.

'There is something else, Inspector – if you think the Luston man only wanted more money then you'd think the Luston people would have just given it to him to keep him on board.'

'That's true,' admitted Sloan. It didn't work like that in the police force. Police pay scales were fixed and the promotion ladder up them had, in Sloan's opinion, a lot in common with both a greasy pole and the board game snakes and ladders. Alongside any ladders there might be, it didn't need saying, were an awful lot of snakes. And nobody had ever called staying on a greasy pole easy, either. 'By the way, can you tell me anything about a remainder-man?'

'That's easy. It's the one – man or woman – who collects at the end of the day.'

199

'Legally?'

'Usually. Not always, of course, because perfidy takes many forms,' the other man informed him kindly, 'and here in the City one way and another we tend to come across it quite often.'

If there was one thing Detective Inspector Sloan didn't like it was being made to feel a country bumpkin. 'I daresay you do, but I don't suppose you have as many cases of murder in your line as we do,' he said, before thanking the man and ringing off.

CHAPTER TWENTY

Detective Constable Crosby had planted himself down in front of Sloan with a noticeable lack of ceremony, returning rather in the defensive manner of a worker bee that hadn't been able to find any pollen on a rainy day. 'I'm starving, sir. Isn't there a law about a worker having to have a break for food every four hours?'

'Quite possibly, Crosby, but I'm not sure if the police are workers within the meaning of the Act,' said Sloan calmly. 'All the same I'll have your report before you head for the canteen if you don't mind.'

'In the matter of crumpled wings,' said Crosby, tugging his notebook out of his pocket, 'Ralph Iddon over at Luston has two cars, neither of them damaged.' The constable brightened visibly. 'The Roller's a real beaut. He let me sit in it.'

'But not drive it?' said Sloan, seriously alarmed. The thought of the financial consequences of a set-to with Crosby at the wheel of somebody else's Rolls-Royce sent shudders down his spine in the way that an armed robber wouldn't have done.

''Fraid not, sir, but it was lovely just sitting there.'

'I trust you didn't kick the tyres?' Kicking car tyres was a sign that experienced car salesmen took very seriously.

'No, sir. Of course not, sir.'

'Good.'

'They've got the health and safety people back there again, still sniffing around.'

'Good on them,' said Sloan absently. 'Go on.'

Crosby consulted his notebook. 'Then I saw Elizabeth Shelford, the paralysed young woman at Larking. She swears that Trevor Skewis was with her only until half past nine last night.'

'But no later?'

'No, sir.'

'And how long,' asked Sloan, 'would it have taken him to get from her house to the Lamb and Flag at Friar's Flensant?'

'What sort of car, sir?'

'Trevor Skewis's sort, not yours,' sighed Sloan.

'And what sort of driver would he be, sir?'

'Let's say average, normal,' said Sloan, sighing again.

'Not long. He would have had plenty of time to get over to Friar's Flensant and knock the two Tridgells down. And, sir...'

'Yes?'

'Paul Tridgell had told both Tim Cullen and Trevor Skewis as well as Elizabeth Shelford that he and his sister were going to the pub that evening on foot.'

'Had he, indeed?' said Sloan, tapping his pencil on his desk.

'So they knew the Tridgells would be there that evening.'

'And could probably guess the time they would leave,' said Sloan, veteran of many a turn-out fracas in his days on the beat. 'All they would need to know was which pub to watch and Bob's your uncle.'

'Yes, sir. Sir, what's oakum?'

'Tarred rope. Why?'

'When I asked Elizabeth Shelford what she did all day she said she picked oakum.'

'I daresay it's a way of saying that she was a prisoner in her own home.'

'I don't know why because she's got a car.'

'I don't either, Crosby. And after seeing her, where did you go then?'

'I went and saw Simon Thornycroft down by that bridge they're building over the river. He's got a newish Mercedes – the big one – not in quite the same league as the Rolls-Royce but not bad, not bad at all as cars go.'

'I'm glad you liked it,' said Sloan in a tone studiously without inflexion.

'Its front nearside wing was damaged big time but from an earthmover.'

Sloan sat up instantly. 'What?'

'He'd had a bash from an earthmover, sir. There was lots of bright yellow paint from it all over his wing. I checked. And there was a bit of the paint from Thornycroft's car on the earth-mover just like that man said there would be.'

'What man?' asked Sloan, mystified.

'The Frenchman.'

'What Frenchman?'

'Edmond Locard. You know, sir. He's the one who invented the exchange principle that every-one in the detective division is always going on about. The one that says you can't touch any-thing without leaving a trace from you on it or from it on you. Him.'

'I take it,' said Sloan, ignoring this nugget of detection, 'that you also interviewed the driver of the earthmover.'

'No, sir. He wasn't on the site there. Apparently he was needed at the other side of the bridge. The south side. He'd already left by the time I got there.'

'Had he, indeed?' murmured Sloan, making a note. 'So you didn't get his side of the story?'

'No, sir, but I examined the back of the earth-mover even though the driver wasn't there and that's where I found traces of black paint from Simon Thornycroft's car. He'd gone to his lunch early, I expect,' added Crosby. 'The worker, I mean.'

'All right, all right. I can take a hint. You can go and get yours now.'

'Thank you, sir. The canteen's all-day breakfast is very good.'

Sloan nodded. It was no accident that it was always on the menu at the police canteen. Often enough it was breakfast time – that is, the first meal of the day – for some of the force who came in no matter what time of the day or night it was. 'Then after you've had it, we'll go over to Berebury Pharmaceuticals and have a word with Mr Jonathon Sharp.'

'Yes, sir,' he said. 'And, sir, there was something else.'

'Well?'

'I think that man Skewis is a bit sweet on the girl in the wheelchair.'

Or consumed by guilt, thought Sloan. It was a thought though that he was keeping to himself.

For the time being anyway.

'Do come in, gentlemen,' said Jonathon Sharp as a secretary ushered the two policemen into his office at Berebury Pharmaceuticals and showed them to their seats, Crosby at least duly fed and watered.

Detective Inspector Sloan couldn't quite decide what was different about this second interview with the chairman of the firm but very different it was. Then it came to him. The amiable man whom he had first met, relaxed and at ease in his own home just after Derek Tridgell's funeral, was nowhere to be seen here in his office. Instead there was a brisk captain of industry sitting opposite him across a businesslike desk, trying hard to make it clear to the police that every minute counted. To him, anyway.

'Yes,' Jonathon Sharp admitted at once, 'I took on Chris Honley. His coming here had been in the pipeline for quite a long time – ever since the bad news about Derek Tridgell's prognosis got out, in fact.'

'Rather odd that, all the same,' pointed out Sloan, fortified by his conversation with the policeman in the City.

'There's no sentiment in business,' said Sharp. 'Can't be.'

Sloan knew that there was no sentiment in police work either. In theory, that is. In practice, police officers had been known to exercise mercy disguised as discretion. 'And,' he asked aloud, 'how has Paul Tridgell taken it?' Like it or not, that young man seemed to be a key player wherever you looked.

'Badly. Very badly.' Sharp pursed his lips. 'Mind you, he's not the easiest chap in the world to deal with in the first place. His father would have been the first person to say that. Often did, actually, now I come to think about it. Too many chips on his shoulder. At least,' he added, 'Derek never asked me to give the boy a job here. I was really grateful for that, I can tell you.'

Nepotism wasn't something you had to worry about in the force. How Crosby had got past the rigid selection process was another matter altogether, although Sloan was the first to agree that sorting out the muffs and duffs at a very early stage wasn't the easiest of tasks.

'Quite,' he said non-committally. He didn't think young Paul Tridgell would have got very far in the police selection process either. Applicants were subtly riled on purpose to see if they rose to the bait. He didn't think Paul Tridgell would have been able to resist doing that for one moment.

Sloan looked carefully across the chairman's desk now, mindful that here was yet another man who had been at the Tridgell funeral to hear Paul's accusation of a killing, a man moreover whose car the two policemen had just examined in the firm's car park. As well as examining it they had also taken photographs of it, paying attention to quite a lot of damaged paintwork, including that on the front nearside wing, even though this did appear to be rather rusty. With his arm considerably strengthened by this, Sloan said, 'Where were you last night, sir?'

Jonathon Sharp's eyebrows shot up. 'What happened last night, Inspector?'

'There was very nearly a nasty accident,' said Sloan succinctly. 'So where were you?'

The chairman's lips twitched. 'Eating out in what you might call the Calleshire *profonde.*'

'And where is that exactly?' asked Sloan, irritated. He didn't like playing verbal games. Especially in French.

'At Ornum.' Sharp frowned. 'At the Ornum Arms restaurant, actually.'

'Posh nosh,' said Detective Constable Crosby, who hadn't been able to fault the canteen's all-day breakfast.

'They know me there, Inspector...' began Sharp.

'Not alone, I take it?' Sloan asked. To be known by a head waiter cut no ice with the detective branch. They had other measures of worldly success.

'Of course not, Inspector,' said Sharp stiffly. 'I was having what you might call a working dinner with a member of my staff.'

Crosby stirred. 'Lucky them.'

Jonathon Sharp turned his head towards him. 'Sometimes, Constable, it is easier to talk freely outside the working environment.'

'Walls have ears,' observed Crosby to no one in particular.

Detective Inspector Sloan was the first to agree with both of them. In his experience, suspects often found their tongues in the custody suite but just as often lost them again later on in the interview room with their solicitor sitting at their side and a camcorder whirring away. He asked Sharp who his guest had been.

The chairman of Berebury Pharmaceuticals had the grace to look somewhat discomfited. 'Chris Honley.' He hesitated. 'I felt discreet surroundings were necessary.'

'Why?' asked Sloan bluntly.

'I was asking him what he'd found particularly important after he came to us. You will understand that there has been a bit of a hiatus here since Derek fell ill.' He sighed. 'He was such a good man, you know.'

'And presumably,' said Sloan in a tone that was studiously neutral, 'you also wanted to know exactly what Honley had left behind at Luston Chemicals.'

'I already knew some of that, Inspector.'

'But not all?'

'Naturally Honley was bound by a confidentiality agreement with his former employers.'

A barely suppressed snort escaped Crosby's lips. 'Pull the other one,' he muttered only just under his breath.

'It's true,' protested Sharp awkwardly. 'There are facts and other facts in our line.'

It was simpler in the police force, thought Sloan to himself. There were known facts and unknown facts in a case and in his book there was information that had been verified to court standard on the one hand and there was conjecture and speculation on the other. Separating the wheat from the chaff was what took a case forward. The converse was that failure to do so held it back in no uncertain way.

'About the car in your parking place, sir...' said Sloan.

'That's not my car,' said Sharp immediately. 'It's my wife's.' He rolled his eyes. 'I know it's a bit bashed about but she's not the best driver in the world. We have it done up again every now and then but it's no use her having a new car. It's not too bad to be on the road, is it?'

Detective Inspector Sloan, Head of the CID in 'F' Division said that the roadworthiness of cars was not his province.

'Some women have pretty poor spatial awareness, you know,' said Sharp.

Detective Inspector Sloan did know that but felt it was as much as his life was worth to say so in some quarters, notably anywhere within the hearing of female Police Sergeant Perkins. Known in 'F' Division as Pretty Polly, she could be more than forthright in anything touching on the comparative abilities of men and women.

'It's the supermarkets,' sighed Sharp. 'She needs more space and they don't always have it in their car parks.'

'And your own car, sir?' asked Sloan, undiverted.

'Mercifully she doesn't drive that one. Says it's too big for her.'

'I meant where is your own car now?'

'Having a new gearbox fitted.'

'Since when?'

'Since the day before yesterday. Is it important?'

'Could be,' said Sloan. 'When did you get back from Ornum last night?'

He frowned. 'About ten. Honley didn't want to say too much. He said it was a bit soon to come to any conclusions about anything in our firm until he'd picked up all the threads.'

'Surprise, surprise,' muttered Crosby from the sidelines.

'I take it your wife can confirm the exact time you got home,' said Sloan, not very hopeful. Even when sworn, the evidence of wives was not always considered sound by those involved in law enforcement.

Pour cause.

Jonathon Sharp came back with surprising swiftness. 'I'll say she can. She was a bit cross, actually. I interrupted her ladies bridge when she was playing a risky three no trumps with a singleton heart.'

Detective Inspector Sloan put his notebook away. 'Thank you, sir. That's all been very helpful.'

It was only when they were back in the police car that Detective Constable Crosby, still very much a bachelor and no player of the game of bridge, turned to him and asked, 'What's a singleton heart, sir?'

CHAPTER TWENTY-ONE

In many workplaces the advent of Friday afternoon betokened an almost palpable lowering of tension. As often as not, the big bosses had already headed off for long weekends in the country while lesser mortals compiled lists of unfinished work under the heading of what needed to be done first thing on Monday morning. Having thus metaphorically – if not actually – cleared their desks they then either joined colleagues for a lunch break more prolonged than usual or foregathered after work to complain about the frailties of their bosses.

It wasn't like that at Berebury Police Station. Already members of the uniformed branch were beginning to report for late duty since these days Friday nights on the streets were nearly as demanding as Saturday nights. Anyway, as far as Superintendent Leeyes was concerned, the weekend didn't really begin until he stood on the first tee of Berebury Golf Course on Sunday mornings. He always held as he stood there, number one wood in hand, ball on tee, that detection had no time boundaries.

'My view, Sloan, is...' he was saying now – and at length.

Detective Inspector Sloan had long ago decided that there was only one thing to do when the superintendent was pontificating and that was to appear to be listening attentively. Any other course of action was ill-advised since his superior officer had a tendency to stop suddenly and make sure that all those present were paying attention – usually just as the thoughts of his listeners had started to wander.

'Don't you agree, Sloan?' he barked presently.

'Er – yes, sir, of course, sir,' said Sloan hastily, hauling his thoughts back from trying to decide exactly where he was going to plant a new floribunda rose in his garden. There was a spot just inside his front gate that needed a bit of colour... 'Very important, sir.'

'No stone should be left unturned.'

'Certainly not, sir,' said Sloan, pulling his thoughts back with a jerk. 'Or avenue unexplored,' he added to himself.

'Or avenue unexplored,' said Leeyes aloud. 'So I agree that the only realistic course of action left for you to take now is to go out to the bridge-works and interview the driver who hit Thorny-croft's car. You'd better tell Calleford Division that you're going there. Strictly speaking the south end of the bridge is in their manor.' He grimaced. 'Professional courtesy and all that.'

'Of course, sir,' said Sloan, only too aware of the view the superintendent took of any invasion of his own territory. He coughed and went on, 'We've already checked that the man who was driving the earthmover is still over there and that Jonathon Sharp's car was indeed in the garage having a new gearbox fitted at the material time just as he said.' There was someone else he wanted to see but he didn't say this to the superintendent.

Leeyes grunted. 'There aren't any other loose ends that I can see, more's the pity.'

'What we can't do, sir,' went on Sloan regretfully, omitting any mention either of something else that had occurred to him to check, 'is to watch Paul Tridgell for twenty-four hours a day, even though I'm sure he holds the key to the whole situation. I'm planning to interview him again first thing tomorrow morning – he should be feeling a bit better by then – but I don't hold out much hope of getting anything more out of him.' He paused and then said, 'After that, sir, I'm afraid we appear to have come to a full stop.' The spectre of the Ponzi scheme at Pelling was already beginning to raise its ugly head.

Leeyes grunted again.

'It seems, sir, that all we can go in for now is masterly inactivity.' It was an expression Sloan's old station sergeant – that incomparable mentor – used to use when he couldn't quite decide what to do next. 'Watchful waiting' was another such.

'Or wait for someone to make a false move,' said Superintendent Leeyes neatly, 'which comes to much the same thing.'

'It would help,' agreed Sloan.

It was not long after that when Detective Constable Crosby turned the police car in the direction of the south side of the River Calle. He was exhibiting a noticeable lack of enthusiasm because, once out of Berebury, the roads on the south side of the river were a jumble of winding country lanes created by years of old track ways, of farms expanding and declining, of neighbours disputing boundaries and of awkward-sized inheritances.

'I expect,' said Sloan sympathetically, 'that they'll build new roads over here when the bridge is finished.'

'I sure hope so,' said Crosby, slowing down and changing gear for a corner that could well have had its origins as the boundary of a Norman manorial holding. 'About time, too. All we need now is a flock of sheep on the road.'

'All we need now, Crosby,' said Sloan with some asperity, 'are some real live clues to what Derek Tridgell meant. If anything, that is. It might just be that his mind had succumbed to all the drugs he was on.' Sloan voiced this, though, without believing it. At the back of his own mind he was still aware of a little anomaly in what had been said to him. He couldn't quite account for it and that worried him: there had been something that didn't quite tie up which, try as he might, he couldn't pin down. There was, though, something he could do. 'When we get back to the station, Crosby, I want you to set up a meeting with the treasurer of the Larking village hall.'

'Yes, sir. Soonest, sir.'

As the car rounded the bend the beginnings of the rising brickwork of the new bridge came into view. Crosby said, 'The work's much further forward on this side of the river, sir, than the other, isn't it?'

'It's because it's sunnier on the south side,' said Sloan.

'Really, sir?'

'I was joking, Crosby.'

213

'Yes, sir. Sorry, sir.'

Deciding not to say anything about looking to their muttons, further mention of sheep being likely to be misconstrued, Sloan reminded the constable that what they were looking for was an earthmover driver called Charlie Barton. 'Sent over here this morning from the north end but we don't know why. Or by whom.'

Charlie Barton wasn't sure either. 'I just got a message to get over to the south side and check that the machine here was in good nick and ready for action because it was going to be needed first thing on Monday morning.'

'And is it?' asked Sloan with a well-concealed forensic curiosity. 'I mean, in good condition.'

'It looks OK to me,' growled Charlie Barton.

'And is it going to be needed on Monday morning?' asked Sloan even more pertinently.

'Search me. I haven't got my orders for next week. Why?'

Sloan produced his warrant card.

'A detective inspector asking about a little bump to a posh car on a building site?' exploded Barton when he saw it. 'What do you think I am? Stupid?' His lip curled. 'So it's all going to be my fault, is it? That's the trouble with the big boys. They make sure they're always on the winning side and that they never get the blame whatever happens.'

'Not necessarily,' said Sloan when he could get a word in edgeways.

'I can see where this is going,' swept on Charlie Barton bitterly. 'By hook or by crook, that man over there is going to get the firm to pay for his

214

repair. I know, I know. Well, all I can tell you is that I don't even know when it happened. I didn't feel a bump or anything.' He hunched his shoulders and jerked his thumb in the direction of the giant earthmover. 'You don't when you're sitting in the cab of one of those beauties. I didn't know anything about it at all until the geezer started banging on my cabin door and shouting at me. Mind you, these big old beasts are pretty sturdy and I daresay his precious car isn't.'

'Could be,' said Sloan pacifically.

Charlie Barton waved an arm in the direction of the earthmover. 'But these are too big to miss unless you're really travelling.'

'Or not looking where you're going,' contributed Crosby.

'Heads in the clouds, some of the big bosses,' muttered Barton. 'All they do is pore over pieces of paper. They need to come down to earth sometimes.'

'He did say it was you who was moving,' pointed out Sloan. 'Reversing, actually.'

'Did he now?' said the man sarcastically. 'Well, I didn't feel him or hear him myself but then I wouldn't, would I? Not in one of these. They make enough noise on their own as it is and they make you wear ear defenders into the bargain.'

'True,' said Sloan, nodding in agreement.

'Should have gone to Specsavers,' concluded Detective Constable Crosby, thus demonstrating, if nothing else, his own susceptibility to the power of modern advertising.

CHAPTER TWENTY-TWO

Kate Booth had made an early start the next morning, knocking on the Thornycrofts' front door in Berebury with her usual vigour. She was rejuvenated by its being a Saturday and thus a holiday from scrutinising other people's draft annual accounts. She was barely recognisable as a qualified accountant today. Gone were the businesslike suit and long-sleeved white blouse. In its place she was wearing a scruffy shirt and well-worn and not very clean trousers.

Her knock was answered by young Lucy Leaton. 'My *faux pas* has gone out,' announced the girl.

'Who?' asked Kate Booth blankly.

'Daddy. I'm supposed to call him Daddy but he isn't my real daddy.'

Kate Booth's brow cleared. 'Oh, you mean Simon.'

'He went out early. Something to do with hiring another car while his is mended.' She turned. 'Mummy's in the kitchen. I'll get her for you. Mummy...' she called out.

'Who is it, Lucy?' a voice came from behind her. 'Oh,' smiled Amelia Thornycroft, 'it's you, Kate. Do come in. You've called to collect some spare caving kit, haven't you? Simon said he'd left it out in front of the garage for you to pick up as he wasn't going to be here when you came. An earth-mover backed into him yesterday on the North

216

Bridge site and he's taken my little car into town to try to hire a car while his is being repaired.'

'Bad luck.'

Amelia laughed, her eyes dancing. 'I must say he put it a bit more strongly than that but you know what men are like with cars.'

'They're their babies.' She grinned. 'Men are babies sometimes, too.'

Amelia didn't respond to this. Instead she said, 'Help yourself to the stuff out there and then come in for a coffee.'

Kate Booth shook her head. 'No, thanks, Amelia. I thought I might just give Paul Tridgell a ring this morning and ask him if he wants to come over to Chislet Crags for a bit of abseiling practice. It's a good day for caving – no rain forecast anywhere at all in Calleshire.'

Amelia Thornycroft frowned. 'Kate, haven't you heard? Paul and his sister were knocked down in the road the other night.'

'No! I don't believe it. Poor them.'

'And poor Marion,' said Amelia with feeling.

'What on earth happened?'

'They were on their way back from the pub out there and a car came up behind them and knocked them over.'

'Phew,' she whistled. 'Were they badly injured?' Her distress was evident. 'I do hope it wasn't serious.'

Amelia Thornycroft paused and said thoughtfully, 'Fortunately they're both just very shaken and bruised, though Paul's wrist was badly wrenched. Although it's not broken it must be pretty uncomfortable still. What happened was very serious in one sense, though.'

Kate Booth looked at her interrogatively, eyebrows raised. 'Tell me.'

'Paul's quite sure someone tried to run them down,' she said slowly.

'No! I can't believe that.'

'Unlikely as it sounds, I must say he seems quite convinced.'

'Who on earth would want to do something like that?' asked Kate.

Amelia shook her head. 'I can't imagine myself and neither can Marion.'

Nobody had ever called Kate Booth slow on the uptake. 'Can Paul?' she asked pertinently.

'If he can he's not saying.'

'Amelia, that could be quite dangerous,' she said.

'I know that. And so does Marion.' She shivered. 'I do hope he's being very careful.'

'So do I,' echoed Kate fervently.

Amelia said, 'You know what he's like. He's not the most – what shall I say? – biddable of young men. He's quite hot-tempered and he can be quite difficult.'

Kate Booth grinned for the first time. 'You can say that again. He flies off the handle more quickly than anyone else I know. No caving for him today, anyway,' she said, starting to heft a bundle of equipment into her car. 'Never mind, there's always another day.'

Amelia Thornycroft sighed. 'It's what one always says when something's gone wrong, isn't it?'

Kate Booth, who knew quite a lot of other things that were said in her office by some of her

218

clients in exculpation when wrongdoing had surfaced during her scrutiny of that client's accounts, merely nodded. 'I think I'll have that coffee with you after all, Amelia, and then I'll just pop over to Friar's Flensant to see how they are this morning. Thank Simon for his stuff for me when he gets back, will you?'

Detective Constable Crosby had collected Sloan from the police station promptly at nine o'clock the next morning. He was patently disgruntled. 'None of my mates has to work on a Saturday morning, sir, like me,' he grumbled. 'It's not fair.'

'Life isn't,' said Detective Inspector Sloan, older and wiser. 'It's lesson one, actually.' Now he came to think of it, it was a lesson that he could wish some of the miscreants who caused them so much trouble down at the police station had learnt at their mother's knees. If they had had mothers, that is. Sometimes he wondered if some of them were truly just limbs of Satan. 'And deserts aren't always just,' he added for good measure, some judgements at the Berebury Magistrates' Court still rankling. 'Something else for you to remember, Crosby.'

'I tried the coffee at the canteen this morning instead of tea,' said Crosby, ignoring this and still aggrieved. 'It's rubbish.'

'Stick to tea,' advised Sloan. 'And get me out to Friar's Flensant while you're about it. I need to talk to Paul Tridgell again.' What he really needed was some sort of lead in the case but he didn't say so.

'Yes, sir,' said the constable, engaging gear and

219

nudging the car's nose none too gently into the swirling traffic beyond the police station car park. 'Now, that girl in the wheelchair, Elizabeth Shelford, she knows how to make coffee.'

Mentally, Detective Inspector Sloan chalked up the fact that the girl in question had yet another admirer in Crosby. And that human personality could transcend all manner of disabilities. 'Does she, indeed?' he murmured, his mind more on how much information he would be able to extract from a recalcitrant Paul Tridgell.

'She made a lovely mug of it when I was there. Her mother was teaching that day and her father was away... Did I say that her father works abroad a lot?'

'No, but it doesn't matter. Go on...'

'She can move everywhere she needs to in her wheelchair on the ground floor.'

'I'm glad to hear it,' responded Sloan absently, his mind still on other things. 'I wonder,' he mused aloud, 'if she was the driver?'

In spite of being trained never to do any such thing, the detective constable took his eyes off the road and turned to snatch a quick look at Sloan's face. 'Elizabeth Shelford, sir?' He brought the car to a halt for a red traffic light that even he could think of no good reason for jumping.

'Someone was at the wheel,' said Sloan ineluctably.

'You don't mean her surely, though, do you, sir?'

'It's one of the reasons that might explain the closing of the ranks,' spelt out Sloan. 'Simple chivalry, perhaps,' he added, trying to equate the young men who had been in the car that night

220

with knights in shining armour. It wasn't easy.

'I'm sorry, sir, but I still don't understand,' began Crosby, engaging first gear and starting to move off again.

'*Esprit de corps*,' said Sloan. He decided against trying to explain the concept of the honour of the regiment to Crosby and simplified it instead to, 'Not shopping someone else for the general good.'

Crosby's brow cleared. 'I get you, sir,' he said immediately. 'Nobody likes a grass.'

'That,' said Sloan, 'is one way of putting it.'

'But it's not legal, is it? Not helping us with our enquiries.' The constable had tried to study the law as it related to vehicles on the Queen's highway because his professional ambition had always been to join Traffic Division. It was unfortunate for him that Inspector Harpe was equally strongly motivated to exploit every possible loophole to make sure that he didn't do any such thing.

'Nobody has said anything at all,' pointed out Sloan. That he had had further thoughts on the matter, he kept to himself.

There was a long silence while Crosby negotiated a country crossroads. Then he said, 'That could mean that none of them remembers who was at the wheel.'

'True,' said Sloan. 'It's a definite possibility since one way or another they seem to have hit their heads hard but I wouldn't bet the farm on it.'

'Or if they had worked it out since, then they aren't saying,' concluded Crosby, turning the car into a road signposted Friar's Flensant. 'No way.'

'And if they had always known, then they aren't saying so either,' pointed out Sloan.

'Putting her in prison wouldn't do anyone any good,' muttered Crosby. 'If it was her,' he said under his breath.

'Don't let Inspector Harpe hear you say that, Crosby.' Sloan considered explaining to the constable a judicial sentencing policy that embraced the concept of *pour encourager les autres* as well as making the punishment fit the crime and decided against it. He thought the word 'exemplary' might be a difficult one for Crosby to understand.

The constable had been thinking about something quite different. 'If it was her and she could drive, why wasn't she driving all the time anyway? And why isn't she driving now?' he added. 'She's got an adapted car but she only uses it to go to the hospital.'

'Crosby, when a boy asks a girl out for the evening he likes to do the driving.' In spite of himself, the memory of his first jejune invitation to his own wife, a young Margaret, came back into his mind. Even now he could still hear the crashing of the gears as he drove away from her parents' house and the flush that had come unbidden to his cheeks. He chose his next words to Crosby with care. 'It's not the same if she takes him. It wouldn't be romantic.'

'If you say so, sir,' said Crosby, bringing the police car to a halt outside Legate Lodge in Friar's Flensant.

Marion Tridgell answered the door, the blood visibly draining from her face when she saw the two policemen standing there. White-faced, she

222

clutched the edge of the door for support. 'Paul?' she gasped, pleading urgently, 'Please, please don't tell me something terrible has happened to Paul, Inspector, I beg you. I couldn't bear it. Not after everything else.'

Detective Inspector Sloan said that he wasn't aware of anything else having happened to her son. The police just wanted to talk to him again: that was all.

'You can't, Inspector. He's not here,' she wailed, losing her rigid self-control for the first time in months. 'That's why I'm so worried. When I called out to him this morning that his breakfast was ready he didn't come down so I went up to his room and,' here she broke down completely, 'he wasn't there. His room was empty.'

CHAPTER TWENTY-THREE

'What about your daughter?' asked Detective Inspector Sloan swiftly. 'Is she here?'

'She's in bed still and fast asleep, thank God,' said Marion Tridgell. 'Dr Browne gave her something to help her settle down after what has happened and she hasn't woken this morning yet.'

'What about the car?'

Her face was a picture of misery. 'It's not in the garage, Inspector. I looked there as soon as I saw that Paul wasn't here. It was his father's car but Paul's been using it ever since ... ever since he came back home.'

'We need to see his room,' said Sloan at once, telling Crosby to put out a general call for the vehicle.

'But I told you, Inspector,' said Paul's mother, 'that he's not there.'

'Nevertheless, madam, we must see his room,' insisted Sloan, stepping past her and making for the stairs. Reaching the bedroom, he crossed to the bed and thrust his hands between the sheets. They were still faintly warm. He glanced quickly round the room and turned to ask Marion Tridgell what her son had been wearing the day before.

She pointed wordlessly to some garments loosely strewn over a bedside chair.

'So what's missing from his wardrobe, then?' he asked.

Marion Tridgell thumbed rapidly through the clothes hanging there. 'Only some old things, Inspector,' she said. 'His trekking gear. I know that that was all there because I'd washed everything when he got back from Brazil and hung it all up in here.'

'And his shoes?' Detective Inspector Sloan wasn't going to let his own wife, Margaret, wait on their son hand and foot like that. When the boy got to Paul Tridgell's age he could do his own washing. And he, his father, would see that he did.

'His trainers aren't here.' She looked unhappy. 'He wears them all the time.'

Sloan looked round the room again. 'Anything else missing?'

'His mobile,' she gave an anxious smile, 'but

then he never goes anywhere without that. The young don't, do they?'

'So have you rung him on it?'

'It was the first thing I did, Inspector. I tried again and again but it wasn't switched on so I left a message.' She said, 'I think they call it voicemail but I'm not sure.'

'The number, please?'

'But...'

They were interrupted by the sound of a knock on the front door. 'Excuse me, Inspector...' Marion hurried down the stairs while Sloan took another look round Paul's room. The only thing that was certain was that he hadn't left any note there.

Kate Booth was standing at the door. 'I've come to see Paul,' she said to Marion. 'I've just heard about the accident...'

Detective Inspector Sloan came down the stairs just as Crosby came back from requesting traffic to look out for Paul Tridgell and his car. 'Number recognition are searching for the car now, sir. He can't have gone far.'

Kate Booth looked from one man to the other. 'Paul? Gone where? I thought he'd been injured.'

Marion Tridgell, looking older by the minute, said tremulously, 'I think someone hoped he had been.'

The accountant's eyebrows shot up. 'Not me, anyway,' she said. 'I'd promised to take him over to Chislet Crags for a bit more abseiling practice this morning.'

'More?' barked Sloan unexpectedly. 'You've done it before?'

'Rather, Inspector. He's quite keen these days although I must say he never used to be. He's still got all his father's caving gear.'

Sloan stiffened. 'His father's caving gear, did you say? Where is it?'

'In the garage,' said Marion faintly.

Kate Booth was still standing on the doorstep when Sloan shot outside past her and wrenched open the garage door. Marion and Kate followed him. It was quite empty save for a large green lawnmower.

'No caving gear here,' pronounced Sloan flatly, looking round.

Marion clutched Kate's arm and said, 'Look! All Paul's snorkelling stuff's gone, too, Kate.'

Detective Inspector Sloan, Head of CID at the Berebury Division of the Calleshire County Constabulary, had heard other people talk about a light-bulb moment but he had never experienced one himself.

He did now.

'Crosby, the car,' he ordered as he snapped into action. He pointed to Kate Booth, 'You, miss, get in the back. Quickly.' He turned and called over his shoulder to Marion Tridgell, 'We'll be back.'

The constable was already driving out on to the road before he asked, 'Where to, sir?'

'Chislet Crags, of course,' said Sloan swiftly. 'And hurry.'

That Saturday morning was different at Elizabeth Shelford's house, too. For one thing her mother was at home all day, it being the weekend, and thus Mrs Shelford was enjoying a respite from her teaching duties.

'I'm heading for the shops, Elizabeth,' she said, coming into the kitchen, shopping bags in hand. 'Why don't you come with me? It'll do you good to get out a bit.'

'No, thanks, Mum,' she said, starting to back her wheelchair away from the breakfast table. 'Anyway, I haven't got all that much spending money these days.'

'I do wish you'd get out more. We could have a coffee in town and it's not difficult to get you into Berebury now that you've got that adapted car.'

'I'm fine here, thank you.'

'Strangers don't stare at people in wheelchairs any more you know if that's what's bothering you.'

'It's not that.'

'Well, what is it then?'

'I'm not ready for it yet.'

'And when will you be?' demanded her mother. 'Or aren't you going to tell me that?'

'Next year, perhaps. I'm not sure. We'll have to see.' She braced her shoulders. 'But you can't make me and neither can anyone else.'

Mrs Shelford sighed. 'I really don't know what to make of you, Elizabeth. I really don't. And you've been so good about your injuries.'

'I can cope with those.'

'You should always go out when you can,' said her mother, reverting to her original point.

'I'm always going out to the hospital and that's quite enough, thank you.'

'It isn't enough. You know that perfectly well,' she said, exasperated. 'You're not stupid.'

'I can't choose whether I go to the hospital, can I?' Elizabeth said mulishly. 'I can choose whether I go out anywhere else. And I have,' she added. 'Chosen, I mean.'

'It's not good that the only other people you see apart from that are those awful lads who were in the accident with you,' persisted Mrs Shelford. 'They will keep coming.'

'They're my friends.'

'And they'll soon be your only ones if you don't make the effort to go out more and meet other people.'

'They've been very good,' said Elizabeth obliquely.

'Are you staying in because they're coming this morning when I'm not here?'

'No.'

She wasn't listening. 'Who is coming this morning, anyway?'

'I don't know, Mum. Honestly. I never do.'

Mrs Shelford barely suppressed a snort.

'It won't be Paul, anyway,' said Elizabeth. 'He said he's got something to do. Something important, but he didn't tell me what it was. He did say he'd tell me afterwards, though.'

'Him!' Mrs Shelford's opinion of Paul Tridgell was not high. 'And what about the other two or is it three?'

'Two. We didn't really know Danny Saville before and he doesn't come. Besides, his leg's still bad.'

'Them, then,' said her mother. 'Those two others.'

'Trevor and Tim?'

'Trevor and Tim,' Mrs Shelford sighed. 'I expect they'll be round here the minute my back's turned.'

'They're both working today,' said her daughter with dignity. 'Hotels and pharmacies are open Saturdays, remember.'

'They don't ever come if I'm here.' It was Mrs Shelford's continual complaint. 'They never do.'

'I'm not surprised,' Elizabeth retorted. 'They don't like the way you go on questioning them, Mum, when they do come here.'

In the ordinary way, the premises of Berebury Pharmaceuticals were deserted on Saturday mornings, save for a caretaker. Not this Saturday. Their new employee, Chris Honley, Chief Scientist, was there. True, he wasn't wearing a lab coat or giving any other sign of being at work but he was there all the same.

Waiting for Jonathon Sharp.

The chairman arrived soon enough and not in a particularly good temper. 'What is it, Honley?' he asked impatiently. 'I'm due on the first tee soon for a four-ball. Saturday mornings on the course aren't as crowded as they are on Sundays.'

'It won't take a minute but I didn't like to ring.'

Sharp sat up. 'You've had a breakthrough with Project Resurgence?'

'Not exactly.'

'Like that, is it? Well, what other holy grail have you found? Tell me.'

'I don't think that's quite the way I would describe it.' Chris Honley was essentially a humourless man and it showed now.

229

'Go on.'

'More something that Derek Tridgell saw fit to keep in a safe place.'

'Well?'

'It's a memo from you to him, actually. Handwritten.'

Jonathon Sharp sat very still.

The other man went on, 'It was telling Derek Tridgell how you wanted to handle that meeting you were going to have with Ralph Iddon and Michael Linane over at Luston Chemicals.'

'Oh, that,' said the chairman with apparent nonchalance.

'That,' said Honley.

'And you say that Derek kept it?'

'In a locked file.'

'I don't see why. It wasn't all that important. It was just an outline plan for our time there, that's all. I wanted him prepared.'

'Exactly. It states that you wanted to collar Michael Linane on his own afterwards, assuming that you'd got nowhere with Ralph Iddon.'

'Nobody ever gets anywhere with Ralph Iddon. You've worked there and you know that.'

'And Michael Linane worked there, too,' said Honley. 'He'd been a friend of mine for ages.'

'What about it? There was a great deal hanging on the outcome of our dialogue with them. You know that, too, Honley. We weren't talking loss leaders in the grocery aisles.'

'Sure. Not as much as actually hung on it as it turned out.'

'I don't get you.'

'This memo instructs Tridgell to make himself

scarce after the meeting and leave you to have a quiet word with Michael Linane, if you could get hold of him.'

'What if it does? I knew we wouldn't get any-where with Ralph Iddon anyway. He's a tough cookie and Michael Linane would never have talked to me in front of him. Never. It would have been as much as his job was worth anyway to be seen talking to me at all after that sort of meet-ing, so I thought if I could just bump into him in a corridor I could say my piece.'

'Which was?'

'I thought he might have been more amenable on his own.'

'A job offer?'

Jonathon Sharp began to bluster. 'I wouldn't have put it quite like that.'

'How would you have put it, then?' Chris Hon-ley sounded a very different man today from the dispirited one lurking in the shadows of garden-ing leave.

'I thought he might just have proved amenable to the odd suggestion about keeping the price of Mendaner up for a while – to give us time to re-group, so to speak. That would have been a great help to Berebury Pharmaceuticals.'

'You must have followed Linane after he left the chairman's office.' Chris Honley sounded quite implacable now.

'I did.'

'So?'

'So I missed him.'

'That didn't come up at the inquest.'

'There was no need for it to since I didn't find

him. I thought he'd be going back to his own office but he didn't go that way and I lost track of him in all those corridors. He must have gone through from the offices into the works part before we left Iddon's office.'

'Which wasn't his territory at all,' said Honley. 'He was Head of Sales. There was no call for him to be there at all.'

'True.' Jonathon Sharp said, 'You'll have to believe me. I never saw him after he left Iddon's office. Now, I must go. I'm late already – and Honley, don't try making bricks without straw. It could be dangerous.' At which point the chairman of Berebury Pharmaceuticals got up and left.

But he didn't go to the Berebury Golf Course.

CHAPTER TWENTY-FOUR

Detective Constable Crosby never minded any instruction to get going. He took his latest orders to get a move on quite literally. Soon clearing the minor roads that led away from Friar's Flensant, he achieved the main road in record time.

'Don't hang about, Crosby,' Detective Inspector Sloan told him. 'We want the Calleford road to begin with and then it's open country all the way.'

The constable hadn't needed telling twice. He soon hit a bigger highway still and bumped up his speed.

Kate Booth, bouncing about in the back of the

police car, asked plaintively if someone could please tell her what was going on.

'We're going to have a look at the place where Edmund Leaton died,' replied Sloan over his shoulder.

'Chislet Crags?' she said. 'The Baggles Bite?'

'That's it,' said Sloan tersely. 'There.'

'You can't, Inspector. The farmer won't let anyone go in that particular cave there. Not now.'

'We'll soon see about that,' said Sloan.

'Old Bartlett'll see you coming and stop you,' she insisted. 'He's piled some stones over the entrance and there isn't any other way up to the opening into that cave except through his farm. You can only get your car as far as his farmyard anyway. After that you've got to walk.'

'Then we'll walk,' said Sloan grimly, keeping silent after that. It didn't mean he hadn't anything to say or that he wasn't thinking hard. It meant he was busy putting piece after piece of a mental jigsaw into place. In the way of difficult jigsaws where most of the colours seemed much the same there were still some unfilled spaces. The outline of those missing pieces, if not their exact colour, was becoming clearer to him by the minute. One of them was shaped in his mind by something that the clergyman had said at Derek Tridgell's funeral: 'where there was death there was hope'. Someone had been hoping for a death and a death had happened. He was pretty sure now that the death in question was that of Edmund Leaton.

'Besides, Inspector,' Kate Booth reminded him from the back seat, 'the whole cave has been flooded ever since the roof fall. You can only get so far into it now.'

'I hadn't forgotten,' said Sloan evenly. In fact that was what had convinced him that they were going to the right place. That and a missing snorkel mask. 'Tell me, did Paul Tridgell ever ask you about the death in the cave?'

'Over and over again,' said Kate Booth. 'Especially why I was bringing up the rear that day. Apparently beginners were not supposed to be last in line.'

The scenery began to change as they travelled east, an outcrop of limestone here and there testifying to the likely presence of caves underneath the ground. Crosby slowed the car down as they approached a crossroads.

'Straight ahead,' said Kate. After another mile she sat up and leant forward. 'Take the next turning off to the left. It's quite soon now. Look,' she said, pointing, 'there's the road.'

Obediently Crosby swung the police car onto a lane that was little more than a single dead-end farm track through a narrow valley. Limestone protruded from the hillsides and towered over the road. As the car bumped over the rough surface she said, 'It's not far now. Just round that bend ahead.'

Presently a long, low stone building came into sight. 'That's old Bartlett's place,' she said, pointing to her right. 'Over there.'

Crosby brought the police car to a scorching stop beside two cars that were already there.

As he did so a woman came out of the farmhouse. 'If it's my husband you want,' she said, holding back a sizeable dog at her side, 'he's gone up to the top field with Rover to see to the sheep. There's a ewe there in trouble.'

'Do you know whose those cars are, madam?'

'Never seen them before,' she said, shrugging her shoulders. 'Walkers, most probably, going through to the pub at Curlington. They often come this way Saturdays.'

Detective Inspector Sloan opened his notebook and consulted a registration number. It wasn't a walker's car. It was Derek Tridgell's old one. He snapped his notebook shut again and turned. 'Crosby, get on with finding out who owns that other car as quickly as you can.'

Somehow Sloan felt he already knew whose vehicle it was.

'Yes, sir. Straightway, sir.'

'We'll find Mr Bartlett ourselves then,' he said, turning back to the woman. 'The top field, I think you said.' She nodded indifferently and went back indoors. Sloan turned to Kate Booth. 'Now, miss, which way do we go?'

'Follow me,' she said, hefting her gear onto her back and stepping out. 'This way...'

'Sir,' it was Crosby calling after him from behind the wheel of the police car. 'I can't get a signal here.'

'There isn't one,' intervened Kate, waving an arm. 'It's a dead spot because of all these hills.'

'Then go back down the road until you do get one,' Sloan instructed Crosby swiftly. 'And call for some backup with lights and quickly. Then come after us and tell me. We'll leave a trail. Look sharp, now.'

'Come this way, Inspector.' Kate stepped forward. 'Ordinary walkers don't know where to find the cave entrance but I do in spite of its being blocked off by the farmer.' She shuddered slightly. 'I haven't forgotten the last time I was there.'

Sloan turned his head and looked back down the hill. There was no sign of Crosby now.

'Paul Tridgell knows where it is,' Kate was saying. 'His dad brought him up here once but he insisted he didn't like caving. He told me so.'

Detective Inspector Sloan, shod for urban streets, was already slipping on the grass behind her. The rocky terrain did not make for easy walking either but he followed doggedly uphill in the girl's footsteps. Ten minutes later a slightly breathless Kate Booth came to a halt under an outcrop of limestone and pointed a finger at a bare patch in the grass.

'That it?' he asked.

She nodded.

'You'd never notice it if you didn't know what you were looking for,' he said.

'You weren't meant to,' she said. 'Not after poor Edmund died, anyway.'

They had reached a little overhang under which a hole was now visible. Beside it some stones had been loosely cast aside to reveal an entrance in the ground.

Christopher Dennis Sloan, a one-time keen member of the Owl Patrol of the 3rd Berebury Scout Troop, dropped to his knees to examine the grass round the entrance. Some of the stalks had been recently bent and broken. You didn't need a tracker's badge, he thought to himself, to know that.

'The way in, Inspector,' said Kate, indicating what to Sloan seemed a very small gap in the terrain.

'It's not a very big hole,' he said doubtfully.

'It doesn't need to be,' she said. 'If there's room for your head there's room for the rest of you. One shoulder at a time, mind you. Like cat burglars,' she added.

Sloan had to take on board the fact that you'd only ever find your way in if you knew exactly where to look so he'd dropped empty pages from his notebook to guide Crosby as they'd toiled up the hill.

Kate Booth slipped her caving gear off her back and dumped it on the grass. She got out a hard hat and crammed it over her hair. 'It's always better, Inspector, that any entrance to a cave is inconspicuous. You don't want anyone else going in there by accident, let alone an animal.'

Sloan nodded.

'And you know how boys are,' she said, strapping on a pair of knee pads.

The police knew how boys were if anyone did but what Detective Inspector Sloan was worrying about now was whether anyone had gone in the cave there not by accident but on purpose. The stones had certainly not been removed from the entrance except with intent. And if the bent and broken still green grass in front of it was anything to go by, the removal of those same stones had been very recent indeed.

What he didn't know either was whether one person or two had gone through the hole and if so, together or separately. He slipped out of his jacket, leaving it conspicuously at the entrance to the cave, at the same time slipping a pair of hand-cuffs into his trousers pocket.

Kate was looking him up and down. 'You're going to get a bit grubby, Inspector, and you'll scrape your knees.'

'Can't be helped. I need to get in there and fast.' He left another sheet of paper under a stone beside the entrance. Even Crosby ought to be able to work that out.

'This way.' Kate Booth had already wriggled inside the entrance, a light shining from the lamp on her head. 'It's easy going to begin with but it gets more difficult as the ground slopes downwards. You'll just have to follow me, that's all.'

Obediently, Sloan squeezed through the entrance and, on his hands and knees, followed where Kate led. The light on her head danced about like a will-o'-the-wisp as she advanced further and further under the ground. As she turned a corner ahead of him, Sloan was momentarily without any light, the expression 'Stygian gloom' coming into his mind again and for the first time he appreciated what the phrase really meant: real darkness, unrelieved by any light at all. True, he had a torch tucked in his belt but he had found out the hard way that a man needed both hands to crawl on his hands and knees.

'Mind your head here, Inspector,' she called back to him over her shoulder. 'There's not a lot of room. You really should have had a hard hat on.'

'No time,' he said. And meant it.

'Health and safety would have a fit.'

Sloan said something very disrespectful about health and safety, bizarrely reminded at that moment that he needed to check why they had gone back to Luston Chemicals after so long.

'Any respectable caver would have a fit, too,' she was saying. 'We do have risk assessment when we can, you know.'

They had risk assessment in police work, too, when they could but in Sloan's view proper policing took priority over it whatever his superiors thought.

He felt rather than saw the ground under him start to slope downwards. Kate's boots moved temporarily out of his line of vision as he slowed down to escape spurts of grit coming up towards his face from them. He put his hand up and gingerly felt the low rough roof above his head, something coming back to him from a plea once made by defence counsel. The lawyer had argued that his client couldn't possibly have tunnelled his way into a bank vault because he suffered from taphephobia. The judge had politely asked for the meaning of the word to be explained to the jury. That it was a fear of being buried alive was something that hadn't meant anything to Sloan until today. He understood it now.

'Now, swing round to your right,' commanded Kate, interrupting his morbid thoughts, 'and follow me until I stop. We're traversing a narrow ledge well above the cave now.'

Detective Inspector Sloan wasn't sure if this was something he wanted to know.

'Be careful here, Inspector, and keep as close to

the right-hand side as you can. It's a big drop.'

Sloan suddenly became eerily aware of a deep void to his left even though his range of vision was so limited. And was aware, too, of the sudden drop in temperature that came with an upward draught from a cold place.

'When I tell you,' Kate went on, 'put your right hand out to feel for the rung at the top of a ladder. It's made of iron and it'll be very cold to the touch.'

Sloan inched his way forward until he felt something blessedly solid. What he'd heard about abseiling hadn't appealed to him one little bit even though Kate Booth had insisted that plenty of people did it for fun. He liked his feet to be under him – not at right angles to perpendicular surfaces, however well harnessed.

'Hang on,' she said, suddenly coming to a stop, 'I can hear water splashing.'

Sloan advanced and listened carefully. 'So can I. Can you put your light out?'

Kate dowsed the lamp on her hat in an instant.

'And keep quiet,' he whispered as he crawled forward to try to get a glimpse of the cavern far below them. He could just about make out that there were two figures struggling in the water, the lamps on their respective heads the only indication of where they were. The two lights danced up and down, intertwining like the heads of necking grebes. It soon became apparent to the watchers above that the two people below were not struggling to keep afloat but with each other. One of them had a face covered with a snorkelling mask, whilst the other was brandishing over his shoulder something short and stubby. Its exact nature was unidentifiable in the poor light emanating from the headlamps of the two below but Sloan could see that it was held as a weapon for all that. Unbidden, a lesson on glassing delivered during his training came into his mind: glassing as an offence depended on how the glass was held and how it was swung in the direction of another man. And exactly where it cut his face.

'Move over, miss, and let me pass you,' he whispered. There was barely room for them both on the ledge as it was and he slithered beyond her with great difficulty, Kate shrinking back away from the edge as he did so. He grasped the top of the iron ladder with relief, swinging himself round to get a better grip on it. His feet firmly on a rung, he descended into the greater darkness, guided only by the sound of the water thrashing about below. There was so little light that it was only when he felt his shoes getting wet that he realised he had reached the water level.

He paused then to snap one half of the pair of handcuffs in his pocket onto the lowest rung of the ladder. Then he kicked his shoes off and lowered himself into the water, its coldness momentarily taking his breath away.

He started swimming towards the tussling pair with a vigorous crawl. As he did so, one of the two in the water brought down whatever it was he was holding in his hand in the direction of the head of the other man, who ducked out of range.

Sloan shouted 'Police!' at the top of his voice.

Both men turned their heads and looked towards him, the one holding the weapon immediately dropping it out of his hand and letting it sink out of sight into the water.

'Thank goodness you've come,' gasped one of the figures. 'Paul Tridgell has been trying to kill me.'

The next two things happened absolutely simultaneously. There was a noise from the ledge above and a great spotlight was targeted on the water, illuminating a scene that might have been drawn by Gustave Doré. And at the same time Detective Inspector Sloan became aware of a figure slithering down the ladder towards them. Then he suddenly felt himself being dragged down in the water by unseen hands. His lungs bursting, he kicked out as vigorously as he could, conscious only of a great turmoil in the water above his head and an even greater pressure in his ears. He didn't know how long it was before other hands took over and mercifully dragged him back to the surface and blessed air.

It had seemed an age.

'We've got him, sir,' spluttered Detective Constable Crosby. He had one arm round the neck of a man still in the water and the other round a lower rung of the ladder.

'He nearly did for you, Inspector,' gasped another voice which he dimly recognised as that of Paul Tridgell. 'Me, too, come to that.'

Sloan coughed as he trod water and tried to get his breath back. He pointed speechlessly at the handcuffs dangling from the bottom rung of the ladder. The other two men towed the third man, still struggling, towards the ladder and snapped the man's right wrist into the empty half.

242

He himself also hanging onto the ladder, Detective Inspector Sloan drew enough breath to say, 'Simon Mytton Thornycroft, I am arresting you for the murder of Edmund Leaton.'

CHAPTER TWENTY-FIVE

'Are you quite sure, Sloan?' asked Superintendent Leeyes sceptically. 'I do hope you know what you're doing, arresting that man. We can't afford to have the force getting it wrong.'

'No, sir, of course not, sir. I mean yes, sir.'

The superintendent tapped the report on his desk. 'Why should this Simon Thornycroft want to go and kill a man like Edmund Leaton for?'

'His wife,' said Sloan pithily.

Leeyes grunted. 'Like that, was it?'

'She's a very beautiful woman still, sir.' Actually Sloan had to admit that Amelia Thornycroft hadn't looked at her best when he had last seen her. That was when he had interviewed her after Simon's arrest, but nothing could diminish the glory of that auburn hair or the attraction of that wide open face. Or quell the intelligence behind those piercing blue-green eyes. She had been both sad and shocked at what he had said but it had quite been impossible for him to decide whether she was surprised. What he did have to decide, policeman on duty that he was, was whether or not she was likely to have been complicit in the murder of her first husband.

243

He explained now to the superintendent that he didn't think this had been the case.

'It has been known,' said that world-weary upholder of the law.

'I think, sir,' offered Sloan diffidently, 'that this murder was something just short of a Uriah scenario.' It had been his churchgoing mother who had long ago explained to him that David had arranged for Uriah, husband of Bathsheba, to be put into mortal danger so that the man would be killed and he could then marry his widow. Without any questions being asked, so to speak.

'What on earth are you talking about, Sloan?'

'A death, sir, planned by Thornycroft.' The Bible, Mrs Sloan, senior, had always insisted was a great sourcebook for murder. That this had been in the interests of getting him to go to Sunday school he had only realised much later but what had been learnt there had stuck.

'And how, pray, may I ask,' said Leeyes, sitting back in his chair and sounding at his most Churchillian, 'did he contrive a roof fall in a cave at just the right moment when the man was under it?'

For a wonder Leeyes seemed to have used the right word. 'He's a civil engineer, sir,' said Sloan.

'What's that got to do with it?' asked the superintendent testily.

'He knows about explosives.'

'Explosives?'

'The roof fall wasn't accidental.'

'Explain yourself, Sloan.'

'We think Thornycroft had been down there before and stuck a couple of sticks of small

244

diameter gelignite into the rock face above the Baggles Bite. He knew the way into that particular cave – the cavers had fixed a ladder there to save abseiling down to the bottom of the cave, ready for their great attempt on the Baggles Bite.'

It wasn't an accident that Detective Inspector Sloan had used the plural in what he had said. He'd been talking to – no, listening to – another police officer, an expert in explosives. The man had already been down in the cave wearing a wetsuit, and with breathing apparatus strapped to his back. He had a very powerful waterproof torch with him, too, as well as an underwater camera.

And when he surfaced he'd brought a heavy spanner up with him from the bottom of the cave. 'One of your weapons, Inspector,' he'd said as he handed it over. Even now, forensics were looking for Simon Thornycroft's fingerprints on it.

'It was a very professional job,' the expert had reported to Sloan. 'Not that explosives are ever something for your amateur to play about with and they usually know it. The living ones, that is.'

'The accused was a civil engineer,' Sloan told him. It was something he should have remembered earlier. He knew that now. 'He had explosives on-site and would have known how to set a charge all right.'

'And he planned it well,' conceded the expert. 'I reckon all that he had to do after that was to connect some dark twinflex to the gelignite sticks and hide it up somewhere out of sight until the time came. Then it was just a case of waiting until

245

his victim was well into the tight bit of your Baggles Bite, retire and then attach the ends of the leads to a battery.'

'Which he did,' said Sloan. 'On the excuse that the light in his headlamp had gone out.'

'If you ask me,' said the explosives expert after he had emerged from the caves, shaking himself like a shaggy dog, 'the batteries in his headlamp would have done the job nicely. But as for retiring I should imagine that might have been a bit more difficult down there.'

'Not really,' said Sloan. 'He shouted to the man behind him, a fellow caver called Derek Tridgell, to stay where he was until he got back to him for some new batteries. I daresay he got a move on.'

'I should hope so,' said the explosives man. 'On the other hand he knew exactly how far to crawl away from the site before he untied the ends of the leads and touched the battery terminals with them.'

'He must have taped the flex out of the way somewhere so it wasn't seen,' concluded Sloan. The expert didn't have Superintendent Leeyes at his back, ready to pounce on any loose ends. 'He would have had to have done, wouldn't he?'

'He might have cut a groove out for them in the roof while he was about it,' said the expert. 'No, much better than that – he could easily have scraped a little channel for it in the ground and covered it over with dirt. No one would have noticed anything in those conditions, not with Erebus on his side, which you could say he was down there.'

'Who?' asked Sloan bluntly. He'd never been

246

more aware of being alone than when he was in the dark water of the cave.

'The God of Darkness.'

'Ah, I get you.' Sloan was the first to admit that darkness was only a help to thieves and other ill-doers. Not to the constabulary.

'Son of Chaos,' said the expert.

'You can say that again,' nodded Sloan. Chaos had reigned in the water inside the cave all right. While he had been struggling with Simon Thornycroft, Paul Tridgell had tried diving under the water to grasp the man's legs. Crosby had joined in the melee, clinging onto the bottom of the ladder with one hand and stretching out with the other to grab Thornycroft's arm until it was safely snapped into the handcuffs. Kate Booth had shone the light on them all and then guided reinforcements to the spot.

'Don't overdo the drama, Sloan,' said the super-intendent afterwards from the comfort of his own office. 'The press might like it but the force doesn't.'

'No, sir. Of course not, sir.' Sloan decided against telling him that the real drama had come when he had eventually got back to his own home, Detective Constable Crosby in tow. He had been dry and reclothed by then but with his other trousers soaking wet still. His wife, Margaret, had had to be told the whole story by degrees before she could be reconciled to his suit never being likely to be the same ever again and his shoes lost for ever in a murky pool of water in an underground cave.

'You could have drowned,' she said accusingly.

'I can swim.'

'Just as well, wasn't it?' she said, unappeased.

'I wouldn't have gone into the water if I could help it.'

She gave him a very considered look. 'Really?'

'Of course,' he mumbled.

She raised her eyebrows and asked, 'So what would you have done then if you couldn't? Watch the man kill Paul Tridgell?'

'Well...' he temporised, aware that whatever he said would be wrong.

'I don't think so, Christopher,' she said.

Neither did Sloan but he was old enough and experienced enough not to dwell too long on the 'what might have happened' side of life.

Or to argue with a wife struggling with the conflicting emotions of anger and relief.

Margaret Sloan next trained her guns on a still slightly damp Crosby. 'And what about you, Bill? Can you swim?'

'No, Mrs Sloan.' He shook his head, his hair nowhere near dry after a shower. 'But I didn't have to. You see all I had to do was to hang onto the bottom of the ladder and grab the accused while the inspector and Paul Tridgell dragged him over.' Referring to a man as 'the accused' stripped him of status quicker than anything else that Crosby knew.

'Well, don't do it again either of you,' she said, relaxing at last.

'Oh, I shan't,' said Crosby earnestly. He looked downcast then and said, 'I don't suppose I shall be allowed to ever again, anyway.'

'Why not?' she asked.

'Control had told me I wasn't to go down into

the cave until they'd made sure it was safe to do so and their backup arrived.'

'Oh, they did, did they?' she said dryly.

'But when the computer said the other car belonged to Simon Thornycroft I thought I'd better get down there, pretty pronto. I'll probably,' he forecast gloomily, 'get a real rocket for disobeying orders when I get to the station in the morning.'

CHAPTER TWENTY-SIX

'I've always known Dad was uneasy about something, Inspector,' said Paul Tridgell. He was back in his own home, safe and sound now, although his mother had taken a lot of convincing of the fact. He had an even bigger bandage on his right wrist today and hadn't hesitated to swallow some painkillers. 'But I didn't work out exactly what – until yesterday, that is.'

'After Thursday night's car accident?' hazarded Sloan.

'It was no accident,' said Tridgell feelingly. 'Once I'd got that into my head I started thinking.'

'And?'

'I'd already worked out that it had to be either Jonathon Sharp or Simon Thornycroft.'

Detective Inspector Sloan didn't see any reason to tell him that he, too, had got as far as realising that days ago. What had let Jonathan Sharp off the hook as far as Sloan was concerned had been a phone call to health and safety after he had heard from Crosby about their second visit to Luston Chemicals.

It appeared that another employee had nearly ended up in another of their vats. 'A design fault in the protective mechanism,' one of their examiners had reported to him. 'It wasn't so obvious the first time but we should have spotted it all the same. It was still death by misadventure though,' he had added as if the right inquest verdict was what had mattered.

Business wars had mattered at Luston, too, but it wasn't them that had led to murder. Consciously leaving two firms to fight their own battles, Sloan had turned his mind in another direction.

What had first led him to Thornycroft was something quite different: the tiniest of discrepancies in what had been said and what had not been said. Kate Booth had spoken of a great bang in the cave, Simon Thornycroft of a whoosh: Kate of the distinctive smell of marzipan after the explosion, something Thornycroft had failed to mention, even though their police expert had said it would be there and noticeable.

'And then?' he asked Tridgell now.

'I realised that whoever had been at the wheel of that car outside the Lamb and Flag was trying to prevent me – what is it you lot call it? – "pursuing enquiries".'

'We'd reached that conclusion, too, sir,' said Sloan gravely. He hadn't thought that the day would come so soon when he would feel happy about calling young Paul Tridgell 'Sir' but boy had turned into adult as swiftly as any maturing chrysalis. He decided against arguing about Tridgell's referring to the police as 'you lot'. They had, after all, been called worse.

'Then it dawned on me that when Dad kept on saying "Dammit, dammit" he wasn't swearing. He was telling them to try to dam the water in the cave while they were trying to get to Edmund Leaton.'

'Just so,' said Sloan, who hadn't forgotten any of Derek Tridgell's last words. It was 'the wrong remainderman' who had given him the most cause for thought. It had only been when Kate Booth had said that as a complete beginner at the time she was the wrong caver to be bringing up the rear of their little party that day – it was usually the most experienced one who went last – that he had worked it out. It should have been Simon Thornycroft there but Thornycroft needed to be just behind Edmund Leaton and have Derek Tridgell immediately behind him to come back ostensibly for spare batteries.

'So I decided to take action,' said Paul Tridgell.

'Don't do it again,' said Sloan automatically.

'But what I couldn't understand was why Dad let things rest like he did.'

'He might have felt he was in danger if he had taken any action,' suggested Sloan.

'He wasn't that sort of man,' said Paul, stoutly defending his father for the first time in his life. 'He wasn't a coward.'

Detective Inspector Sloan said, 'He might have felt that as Amelia and Lucy Leaton were being taken care of, that the least said the better

251

in the circumstances.'

'Until he couldn't not say it any longer.' Derek Tridgell's son put it awkwardly but Sloan knew what he meant.

'I am sure he thought he was acting for the best,' said Detective Inspector Sloan.

'And who are we to say he wasn't?' Paul challenged him.

As far as Sloan was concerned, answer came there none.

'I hear you got your man, Seedy.' Inspector Harpe pushed a mug of tea companionably across the table in Sloan's direction. The two of them were sitting together in the canteen at the police station at the end of the week.

'I've got him all right,' said Sloan warmly. 'Whether the Crown Prosecution Service'll get him, too, as you know, Harry, is in the lap of the gods.' Since he had encountered Erebus, God of Darkness, son of Chaos, his view of the powerfulness of the gods had changed.

'Too right.' The traffic inspector's muted response exuded sympathy with this reservation. 'Good work, though, Seedy. I wish I could say the same. I don't think that we're ever going to nail whoever was driving in that fatal at Christmas.'

Sloan took a sip of his tea. 'I've had a few thoughts about that, Harry.'

Inspector Harpe sat up. 'Really?'

'Nothing that you could prove, though.'

'That happens. Go on.'

'Something Crosby noticed put me on to it.'

'Crosby? You're joking.'

252

'No, Harry. Seriously. He sussed out that the girl has had a properly adapted car in her garage for ages, courtesy of her mother's insurance company.'

'What about it?'

'And that she only ever uses it, though, to go to her hospital appointments.'

'Cold feet about getting back to driving?'

In the circumstances that didn't seem a good metaphor. 'Only literally, I suppose,' Sloan said. Actually he had no idea whether the feet of a woman paralysed from the waist down were cold or not.

'So?'

'Not only is she not using the car but she won't go out of the house at all, except as I say to the hospital.'

Inspector Harpe's eyebrows rose in a prodigious frown. 'Why ever not?'

'Doesn't it strike you as odd, Harry, too? She's got a brand-new car specially adapted for her sitting in the garage but she won't go out socially at all.'

Harpe sniffed. 'I'm not all that struck on the social side of things myself, Seedy. The wife likes it, though, more's the pity.'

'You're not a young woman, Harry. Not even a half-paralysed one.'

'Too right, I'm not,' growled the traffic inspector, who had found out the hard way that nowadays some young women drivers were as hazardous, not to say as aggressive, as some young men behind the wheel.

'The village hall in Larking has just had a major

253

refit,' remarked Sloan with apparent inconsequence. 'I started to put two and two together after Crosby told me about Elizabeth Shelford's self-immurement ... well, staying within the house walls, anyway.'

'I thought they only went in for walling up naughty nuns.'

'This is immolation – I think that's the right word – in her own home, not bricked up behind a wall and not in history.'

'All right, all right.' Harpe took a swig of tea. 'Go on, then.'

'When Crosby asked her what she did all the while she was indoors she told him that she picked oakum.'

'They don't do that in prisons any more.'

'Not in prisons, no. Not now. But after Crosby also told me the girl wouldn't go out at all unless she had to, it occurred to me that she might be acting out a theoretical sentence for causing death while under the influence.'

'I don't get it, Seedy.'

'Neither did I, Harry, until I had a word with the treasurer of the village hall out there.'

'I'm still not with you.'

'He admitted that they'd had a sizeable strictly anonymous donation just after Christmas which got them going on the restoration work. Very pleased, he was.'

'Lucky old them.'

'Which sum, funnily enough, was exactly the same amount as the likely fine that a convicted driver would have got in a case of causing death while driving under the influence.'

'I begin to get your drift.' The traffic man nodded his head slowly. 'It adds up, I suppose.'

'Big fine, long prison sentence, and driving ban,' said Sloan checking off one finger after the other. 'She's behaving as if she's had them all.'

'You could be right.' Inspector Harpe drained his mug. Like all policemen and prison officers, let alone psychiatrists and the clergy, he knew quite a lot about atonement and redemption. And remorse. Especially remorse. 'I daresay the others in the car all know, too.'

'They probably think she's suffered enough,' said Sloan, getting to his feet. 'More tea, Harry?'

The publishers hope that this book has given you enjoyable reading. Large Print Books are especially designed to be as easy to see and hold as possible. If you wish a complete list of our books please ask at your local library or write directly to:

Magna Large Print Books
Magna House, Long Preston,
Skipton, North Yorkshire.
BD23 4ND

This Large Print Book for the partially sighted, who cannot read normal print, is published under the auspices of

THE ULVERSCROFT FOUNDATION